One Last Gift
An Anthology

James N. Richardson

As retold by D.F. Hart

Copyright

Copyright © 2019 by 2 of Harts Publishing

Library of Congress Control: Pending
ISBN: Softcover 978-1-7330454-6-9
eBook 978-1-7330454-7-6

Custom Cover Design commissioned for 2 of Harts Publishing by:

Jennifer Givner of
Acapella Book Cover Design

Find her at
www.acapellabookcoverdesign.com

Published 2019 by 2 Of Harts Publishing

www.2ofharts.com

DISCLAIMER

Dear Reader,

The stories you are about to read are just as my father wrote them back in 1994. Save some grammatical corrections, before you are his unedited works.

Because these are unadulterated 'from-the-heart' stories and deal with such topics as forgiveness and redemption, I feel the need to disclose that the last two stories in the collection do contain some adult content that is probably best suited for those over eighteen years of age.

D.F. Hart, Editor
2 of Harts Publishing

Table of Contents

July 22, 2019

I got a call that changed it all
Two weeks ago today,
And my whole world began to fall
Two weeks ago today.
I rushed to come be by your side
Two weeks ago today,
And learned I had to say goodbye
Two weeks ago today.
My heart was broken, yours set free
Two weeks ago today,
I'll never be the way I was
Two weeks ago today.
If I was given any wish
I know just what I'd say,
I'd ask to turn back time beyond
Two weeks ago today.

- D.F. Hart

Love and miss you, Dad.

Infinity

Life is a storm
Life is a storm
When man stands alone
As a single cloud in the sky

Many look on Him as a sign
Many say of Him words of wonder
Laying alone he faces life
Being alone he faces death

Life is a stormy sea
Life is a stormy sea
Waves high and rough
Winds that have no mercy

Look above for answers below
Life is a storm
Look around which way to go
Life is a storm

Is it love?
Is it money?
Is it fame?
Life is a storm.

Death is a calm
Death is a calm
It brings one full circle
The beginning to the beginning.

The Old Man at the Corner Store

An old man sat looking east out the window of the
      corner store.
He saw people come in.
One bought a pack of smokes,
Another a bag of ice.
A kid was a nickel short for a candy bar.
The old man pitched the kid a dime and said
"Next time you'll have that five cents you need."
The kid never said a word - -
Not "OK!",
Or "Thanks" - -
Not a word.
After the kid left with his candy,
The clerk behind the counter
Remarked, "He should have just said thanks."
The old man just smiled and thought –
(Since no one could see his thoughts)
He will, the next time he helps someone else.
You see, the old man was once was a kid,
and,
Once was a nickel short.

Stonecutter

With the evening sun going down and the light breeze out of the east, I sat looking at a monument man had built to man. This structure was known to many and admired by outsiders as well as townsfolk. During the day the offices inside were always busy and handled the normal day's events, such as the License Bureau drawing up marriage licenses. Of course, the courtroom was always active with unhappy people trying to obtain answers to unanswerable questions from the 'Halls of Justice'. But now, in the late afternoon, the courthouse stood in all its silent splendor. The artist who built the monument many years ago was surely thinking of the art of construction, and not the bustle of everyday government business.

Now with opened eyes I could see the true beauty of man's work; men who have long since gone to their just rewards. Men who did not pre-fabricate or use the excuse of speed to meet a deadline. No, these were men who put life into the silent stone and marble that became a place of beauty, strength, and pride for the residents of Wise County, Texas.

I felt a true need to say, 'thank you', and pray for those hard-working men, for they left behind a part of themselves for all passing by to admire and take pride in.

But this wasn't about the courthouse, per se, but one man who worked, yes, dedicated himself to a project that he, I believed, would have been proud to say he'd been a part of. Although the single man I envisioned as I sat there may not have been real, I was sure that the qualities of at least a few who worked on the courthouse might have been personified in a man I called Wade Gold...

Wade first came to Wise County in a covered wagon and was like most who came this way looking for a fresh start and a future. It was the early 1890's, and Wade was in his mid-twenties, a strong young man over six feet tall who could out-work most teams of three men.

People did not know much about Wade, as he did not say much, but always had a smile on his face and was pleasant to be around. He never talked about his past or where he came from, but even so, folks considered him a nice enough person.

Some of the ladies in town thought Wade a handsome man, quite the catch, but a little hard to approach. And since he was always a perfect gentleman and kept to himself, the ladies had a time trying to catch his eye. Occasionally some would drop a package or a handkerchief in his path. Wade would always stop and render assistance, but always moved on afterward with rarely a word, just a smile and a tip of his hat.

One day while at the dry good store, Wade learned of a town meeting to discuss the building of a courthouse. This would be the most important project ever undertaken by the people of Wise County. They were a new county in a new state, and the new county seat needed a place to conduct business – along with a place to try and hang some of the local and outside troublemakers.

And after all, Decatur was on one of the major cattle drive routes between the Northern states and the big city of Fort Worth, Texas, and such a town needed more than the gambling houses and brothels it had become known for. Decatur needed a courthouse, one that would make its presence known throughout the North Central Texas area – A courthouse built for the future, not just something to get by for the present.

The town already had a jail, and a shell of a building that was used for trials and such. But Decatur, and Wise County, needed a courthouse that would stand for centuries and speak loudly to all who saw it – and proclaim that the people of Wise County had a vision of the future.

All this talk of the new courthouse interested Wade Gold very much. While he was now a farmer and worked with livestock, his past was bedded deep, and though he would like to have forgotten most of his past, some of it he remembered fondly. Pleasure in working hard and building things that would last many lifetimes.

When the meeting was held, everyone in the county turned out. Men wore their Sunday best, and the women displayed their newest dresses and bonnets. Children played and ate candy; the entire event took on a festive air.

But the real reason soon caught everyone's attention, and the talk began about where to build the new courthouse. This did not last long, and the site was selected by popular vote. Now the talk turned to how the courthouse would be paid for. This was also decided quickly; the project would be paid for through taxes and a bond sale.

Wade Gold's interest peaked when the talk turned to what to build the courthouse out of. Some said pine, others, oak, still others suggested stone from the nearby hills of Wise County. Wade, being a soft-spoken man, gained every ear in the crowd when he said, "Granite, and marble." He then explained how these building materials would last forever and told of their beauty. He fell quiet again as everyone ran his words through their minds.

There were questions. First, how did this quiet dirt farmer know about hard stone? Where would these stones come from? How much would they cost? And perhaps, the most important question of all: Who had the knowledge to work with such materials?

Two of the questions were readily answered. It would be brought in from a neighboring county by wagon, and the cost would off-set any other materials because of the length of time the stone would last compared to the other materials suggested. Now – Who had the knowledge to work the stone?

Again, Wade spoke. He had worked the stones before, and now he would reveal some, but not all, of his past. Wade told the people of working back East as a stone cutter and fitter, then offered to work on the project at no cost to the county. The part about no-cost excited the people to the point that where or how his knowledge was obtained became unimportant.

The people had selected a site and chosen what materials to use. Now they gathered names of local men to help with the construction. Amidst the signing up of men would use their wagons to get the stone, and men who would work the stone, the question of Wade Gold's past seemed forgotten.

***

Months passed as the project got underway. Plans were drawn up and fought over as to how the courthouse should look, how many rooms it should have, even a tough-fought battle about the main entrance and where it should be. Someone finally suggested four entrances, one on each side of the building, and since the courthouse would be the center of the town square, this idea pleased everyone. The structure would have four entrances, a basement, and be three stories tall, with the district court held on the top floor. The basement was in case of the dreaded Texas twisters that came through from time to time, thus creating a place of safety for anyone caught away from home during a storm.

With plans drawn and the size of the courthouse agreed upon, the selection of the stones and transporting them to the building site could begin. Wade Gold was asked to lead the selection team and would travel to the neighboring county to choose the stones. Wade knew how the people felt, and this gave him a good idea of what type and color would satisfy the dreams of the county's people. After all, dreams were what brought most of them to this area in the first place.

Don Wilson was a good example. Back east, he worked a black-land farm in Maryland. But he'd always dreamed of being a storekeeper. So, he sold his farm and moved to Texas to become the proud owner of the dry goods store. Another example was John Boon. John wanted to be a rancher, and moving to Wise County, Texas from Kentucky was a dream come true, because cattle could graze on the rolling landscape more easily than on the steep sides of the Estill County, Kentucky hills John once called home.

Yes, many came to fulfill their dreams, and were doing just that. The trip was hard, no matter where they came from. But they all said it was worth it, and they'd do it again. Even Wade, who never talked about where he came from or why he came to Texas.

No one knew of the hardships Wade had faced back east, or the reason behind his move. Everyone else talked openly about what they'd left behind, but not Wade, and from time to time townsfolk talked amongst themselves, speculating about his past – a past Wade reflected on from time to time. A past that had taught him at a very young age the true meaning of freedom, and the value of doing a job well.

But this job, unlike his past, would be done to satisfy *him,* not the people who held him and his family for so many years in the stone pits where Wade had learned, the hard way, the value of life. No. This job was for pride and integrity - and might set Wade Gold free from his past once and for all. This job was Wade's chance to say, through his craft, all that he ever wanted to say to those who made his family's lives a living hell for so many years.

You see, Wade Gold believed that beauty must be built into the project by the artist, the craftsman, before it could be judged as being beautiful by others. This Wade had learned from his father, a true craftsman – a stonecutter from Ireland, who had come to America many years ago with dreams of his own, and who never saw those dreams fulfilled because the price was too high. But Wade could now fill some of those dreams, both for himself and for the memory of his Dad.

***

The construction had begun when Wade and his crew left to select the stones; the ground needed to be cleared and leveled, and the basement dug out. It would take months, even with as many men as there were working on it.

Three months passed before Wade came back to Wise County – three months of sizing and cutting the stones that would form the outside walls of the courthouse. But after three months, all the stones needed had been cut and transported to the site. Now Wade could return and begin the long process of putting the stones into place.

When Wade returned, he discovered more than expected. The construction was going well – in fact, it was ahead of schedule. But Wade also found that a young man by the name of James Wilson, Don's nephew, had been taking care of things at Wade's farm in his absence. James was only twelve, but a very hard worker – a trait he'd inherited from both his parents. His father, James Sr, had taken ill on the trip to Texas and died of fever. His mother, Linda, worked with for her brother-in-law in the dry goods store and made ladies' dresses on the side for extra money.

Linda was in her early thirties, with red hair and blue eyes, and while not what some would call beautiful, her features of womanhood were second to none. Wade had noticed her many times in the dry goods store. Little did Wade know what the future would hold, for himself, for Linda, for James Jr, and for the courthouse.

The afternoon of Wade's homecoming, he arrived and found his front door standing open, a whirlwind of dust flying out from inside his house. As he dismounted, he noticed a broken fence had been repaired, the cow and calf had been moved from the hay field to the new-mended corral, and the barn doors had been fixed as well.

Wade stepped across the threshold to find young James Wilson with broom in hand, working to clear the dust that had collected in three months' time.

"Howdy, Mr. Gold! Momma felt like since you were giving your time for the courthouse, someone needed to take care of your place."

"Is that so?" Wade asked him with a grin.

"Yessir. Besides, the men working on the courthouse won't let me help. They said I'm too young and small and I'd just be in the way."

Wade thought back to his childhood days in the stone yards. At the tender age of 8, his workdays had started at sunup and lasted until after dark.

"James, everyone has a hand in building that courthouse. If you want, I can teach you how to carve the stones."

The boy's eyes lit up as if on fire, and a big smile came across his dust-covered face.

Then Wade added, "But for today, let's get you home. It's getting late and your mother will have your supper ready."

They rode together back to the edge of town and Wade stopped at a small house with a broken front fence.

"Why are you stopping here?" James asked.

"You live here, don't you?"

"Why, yes. But how did you know?"

"I notice things, young man," Wade told him. "By taking notice of things, a man can learn a lot."

Being called a man meant a lot to James and made Wade Gold a special person in his young eyes.

Standing on the front porch was Linda, who spoke to them both at the same time. Wade noticed that Linda had taken her hair down, and it flowed down to the middle of her back. The sunlight caused it to become alive with almost an angelic color, of which Wade took special notice; so much so he almost didn't hear Linda invite him to stay for supper. Being unsure of what he had at home to eat, Wade regained his senses and accepted the invitation.

As he dismounted his horse Linda watched Wade's every movement, paying special attention to the stonecutter's strong arms and long legs. For she, too, had stolen glances at him during his trips into the dry goods store. And as he walked to the porch, she also noticed his long stride and ever-present soft smile.

After washing up for dinner, Wade was served a meal he'd not soon forget – fried chicken, new potatoes and greens, and to top it off, apple pie and fresh coffee. When supper was through Wade and James volunteered to do the dishes; after all, at was the least they could do for such a fine meal. Once the dishes were done and put away, Wade visited, but only for a short time. To stay any longer, he felt, would be improper.

As he rode back to his farm, Wade's mind filled with thoughts of the meal he'd just had, and of James Jr. But most of all his thoughts were of Linda and the way she moved in her kitchen, in full control of all around her. Wade tried to picture the three of them as a family. Could he ever be that lucky, to have a woman as gifted and beautiful as Linda Wilson, not to mention a great son like James?

Maybe. Then again, maybe not.

What did Wade have to offer a woman like Linda? He was poor, barely getting by on his modest 200-acre farm. Land was expensive, up to two dollars an acre, and he had limited funds. The money he did have he'd saved after all those years in the stone yard – money earned with his blood and sweat.

Wade decided that for now, the best decision to make about Linda and James was no decision at all. It was only dinner. Just let nature take its course, if it was meant to be.

Reaching his cabin, he stepped down and unsaddled his horse. Both he and his mount needed rest, and tomorrow he'd start setting the stones for the courthouse. As he prepared for bed, he hoped his dreams would be of Linda.

***

The next morning, Wade rose early, feeling rested. His dreams had indeed been of Linda and James, and Wade felt happy inside for the first time in a long time.

When he reached the building site, he found young James waiting for him. As Wade approached, a few of the workmen asked James why he was up so early, but before the boy could answer Wade spoke up with, "He's my apprentice and will work with me." That quelled any other questions the men might have wanted to ask, and it brought a huge smile to James' face.

The day was filled with excitement for everyone, for all the preparatory work was finished, and now the first stone could be put into place and the true construction of the courthouse could begin. Wade explained to everyone that the first stone was the most important, because if set incorrectly, then all other stones would be out of place as well, so the first stone had to be set perfectly, then all other stones fitted to the first. A team of mules set up on a horse-mill that was hooked to pulleys and a block and tackle rigging would lift the heavy stones into place.

***

Day after day the work progressed. But another event was also taking place that had caught the eye of Wade's co-workers and the townsfolk. Every day at noon, Wade and James Jr's lunch was furnished by Linda. At first, she just brought the lunch then took her leave, but little by little she began to stay with them while they ate, talking about the work and how it was going.

As time went on, Linda found herself looking forward to the noon gathering with Wade. James always had a ton of questions for the stonecutter. Linda always acted as if she wasn't listening most of the time, but Wade was not fooled. So, little by little, he began to reveal his background, in hoped that Linda wouldn't think too harshly of him or his past.

Wade told of coming over to America from Ireland with his father, mother, brother and sister when he was six. He talked about his faith in God, and how he felt that each person was put on Earth for a reason. He shared with her his view that the wicked people in the world had lost their vision of what God wanted them to do, and that was the reason they treated others so badly.

***

Late one afternoon, once the day's work had ended, Wade was invited to Linda and James' home for dinner. After dishes were done, they sat on the front porch of the modest house at the edge of town. Linda began to ask Wade more questions. Before, all the questions had come from young James.

She asked him how he learned the skill of stonecutting and fitting. Wade explained to her that back in Ireland his father, William Henry Gold, was an artist, but after bringing his family over to America he took his art and was forced to apply it to the construction trade, building stone homes in Boston for the city's elite.

After a silent pause, Linda asked, "What do you mean by forced?"

Wade thought for a moment, to weigh his response carefully. Had he gotten to know this woman well enough to tell her the truth about his family, and himself? And after she heard the truth – would she accept or reject him?

He knew one thing for sure. He wanted things to progress with Linda. She'd become his every thought. His daydreams had taken him where he had no right to with her, unless, of course, they were married. He felt he must be honest with her. But would that honesty cost him what he wanted more than anything he'd ever wanted in his life?

Just as Wade began to speak to Linda to answer her questions, James Jr came out to the front porch, complaining of a stomachache. Wade and Linda's attention quickly turned to the young man, who was bent over slightly and holding his midsection. Linda felt James' forehead and detected a slight fever, so she turned to Wade to ask, "Should we get the doctor?"

But Wade had already left the front porch, heading toward the broken gate and the doctor's house. With long, quick strides, he covered the two blocks in record time. After two knocks, the doctor answered and listened as Wade relayed the situation. Doc Buzz, as he was known, wasted no time in getting his bag and walking with Wade back to Linda's house, almost having to run to keep up with the tall, lanky stonecutter.

Wade waited on the front porch for what seemed like hours. As he waited, his mind drifted back to that fateful night in Boston, and another doctor's call to the work house for his dear beloved mother, a victim of consumption. After her passing, Wade's father seemed to lose all will to go on. Wade knew his father blamed himself for the living conditions his family had been subjected to. And for what? "Freedom?" Wade's father had only lasted six months after his wife's death, a tired and broken man.

He remembered his father's last words, apologizing for bringing the family into so much suffering, little to no food, poor housing and bad water, and begged Wade to forgive him for being left to pay the family's debt as bonded servants. That had been the price of passage to America.

People in bondage. Yes. Wade's father had signed to labor in the Boston work camps for twelve years to pay for his family's trip to the new country.

Wade's little brother Joseph, six at the time, was taken in by a Quaker couple in Pennsylvania, and his five-year-old sister Iris was adopted by a family migrating west to forge out a future in Montana. At the age of eight, Wade was forced to remain and settle out his family's debt.

He remembered the hard work. He remembered sleeping in the stone quarry – after all, the master could not have an orphaned boy taking up valuable housing space. He remembered eating out of garbage cans just to stay alive. But most of all, he remembered the beatings. The sting of the master foreman's whip had left its mark on his young flesh – marks his body still carried. He remembered being told he was a white slave and lived and worked as such for twelve long years. Now, he was free, but in a lot of ways still a slave, marked for life.

Wade's memories were interrupted by the opening and closing of the front door. He saw the doctor, leapt to his feet, and without thinking asked, "How's my son?"

The doctor, a puzzled look on his face, replied, "*Your* son?" Noticing Wade's embarrassment at the question, he just grinned and said, "He's going to be just fine. It's a little too much cherry pie for dessert. I'll check on him in the morning." Doc Buzz turned and said goodnight to Linda, who had also come to the front door.

Once the doctor was out of sight, Linda turned to Wade and exclaimed, "Your son? Wade, I didn't know you liked my son so much!"

Wade, looking straight into her deep blue eyes, softly replied, "I feel very deeply for young James." He turned and walked to his horse tied up at the hitching post. As he mounted, he continued, "Very deeply, indeed. As well as his mother. Good night, Linda."

Linda stood on her porch, watching him ride away, trying to think of words to say that would let Wade know just how much she'd fallen in love with him, and how much she wanted to be with him. Soon, he had ridden out of sight and his words still rang fresh in her ears.

As she turned to go inside, she found James standing in the doorway. Her son smiled and asked, "Mom, did I hear Wade call me his son?"

She smiled back at him, nodding her head.

James's smile grew even bigger, and as he turned toward his bedroom he exclaimed, "That's great! That's super! Thanks, God!"

Linda closed the front door behind her and whispered, "Yes, thank you, Lord, very much. Now next time I'll get the answer to my question."

***

Days passed, and the lunches Wade spent with James and Linda continued. Their talk was always light and cheerful, and the setting of the stones was going well. All the men working on the courthouse could sense the finish was close at hand.

One day, as the noon break approached, Wade and several others were setting one of the top stones when the pulley system suddenly gave way, and the large block and tackle came crashing down. Wade jumped up and with his long strong arms pushed the others out of harm's way just as the block and tackle came down, striking him on the back of his head and breaking his right shoulder. The accident also ripped Wade's shirt down the back, revealing his whip-scarred past for all to see. He was carried down from the top floor and to the doctor's office, still unconscious, in full view of everyone at the worksite.

After Doc Buzz began to tend to Wade, the two men who were working alongside him told everyone how he saved their lives. But all their talk didn't stop the whispered questions about his whipping scars. The only time any of the townsfolk had seen marks like that on a white man was when he was a convicted rapist, murderer, or Army deserter – in short, a coward.

But which was Wade Gold? And was that even his real name?

A few even commented out loud that now they knew exactly how Wade knew so much about stonecutting; after all, it was what convicts working on the chain gangs did in prison.

To Linda, having seen the scars and remembering Wade's own words of being forced to cut stone, it seemed to add up. But what had he done to be put in prison? Had she fallen in love with a bad man? Linda was now trying to deal with her feelings.

James, on the other hand, didn't believe for one minute all rumors going around about Wade. He believed in Wade, and would prove, somehow, that the town was wrong. All Wade had ever done was help every soul in town, and James felt the town and its people owed the stonecutter a chance to explain.

But the most important thing to do first was get Wade well. Doc Buzz came out of his office and said he wasn't sure about Wade's condition. "His shoulder will be all right," he told everyone. "I'm just not sure about that head injury – he took a very hard hit, and my knowledge with head injuries is limited. Best thing for him is rest, and prayer."

***

The doctor tended Wade that best he could over the next few days, but he couldn't give Wade the constant care he needed. So, Doc Buzz asked Linda and James if they would take Wade in and care for him.

Linda did not want to at first; what would people say, them not being married? And what kind of man was this who carried such scars? It was through James, and his insistence, that Linda agreed to accept the doctor's request for help. She still loved Wade, but when he finally did wake up, he'd have a lot of explaining to do, and his explanation had better be good – their lives and future were at stake.

The townspeople heard of the doctor's plan to have Wade moved to Linda's house and felt a town meeting was in order. The rumors and hearsay about where and how Wade had gotten his scars had sparked wide concern among many of Wise County's more prominent citizens. As the meeting got underway the sheriff, Bob Stick, a reformed train robber and gunslinger, felt it his duty to place Wade under lock and key until his past could be investigated. Many at the meeting agreed with the sheriff, but just a vote was about to be taken, a friend of Wade Gold's stood and began to speak – a friend Wade never knew he had. A man that was respected all over the county, and who also carried some weight with his profession and social standing.

That man was John Henry Forester, the preacher of the only church in Wise County. People all over had listened to John's sermons at one time or another. He had buried or married or baptized almost everyone or someone they knew in the county, so when he stood to speak, all who were present listened.

John started by asking a question. "Who is Wade Gold? And what crime, if any, had he committed that any among us can say for sure he is guilty of?" The air hung heavy with silence as no one answered.

"And let me know, by a show of hands, the number of people Wade Gold has hurt, or offended?"

No hands were raised.

Then John added, "Let's look at the truth about this man we call Wade Gold. First, he is gifted artist and a hard-working man. He is honest, not given wild women, or drink, not a liar or a braggart."

He paused, looking over the crowd. "Now, by a show of hands, how many people has Wade Gold helped at one time or another?"

One by one, hands went up around the room, and soon only a few were left. Then John added, "I want you to remember who Wade Gold was building this courthouse for," and every soul within earshot now had a hand in the air, as they remembered Wade was working so tirelessly for free.

"You see," John told the crowd, "this lone man with a scarred back has touched all of our lives, and in each case, with love. The kind of love the Bible speaks of, love that is given freely and expects nothing in return. And now you want to lock him up until his past can be investigated? Just how many of us could stand such digging into our past lives?" He stood, silent for a moment, then said, "Let's turn this hanging meeting into a prayer meeting for Wade Gold's return to health."

Suddenly the doors of the meeting room flew open and all eyes flew to Linda Wilson, who was standing in the doorway with a shotgun in her hand and James Jr by her side.

Before anyone could speak, Linda called out, "You people ain't taking my man no damn where and I'll shoot the first person that thinks he'll try. Wade's done nothing wrong, and the only thing he's guilty of is trying to be a good, honest, decent citizen. He's worked hard for you ungrateful people and let his own place go as a result. So, if you think I'm just going to stand by and let you..."

Preacher John interrupted at this point, and some folks chuckled at Linda's expression when he told her, "We were just about to pray for his recovery."

All she could manage after hearing the preacher's words were, "Well...huh...well... Ok, then start praying before I start shootin," then Linda turned on her heel and walked back down the street to her home to take care of the man she loved and wanted.

Preacher John shook his head gently, smiled, and led them all in several hymns and prayers, all on behalf of Wade Gold.

***

Several days passed, with no improvement in Wade's condition. Then one sunny morning while Linda was tidying up the bedroom, she heard a familiar voice say, "Good morning, pretty lady."

She ran to Wade's side and held him in her arms, all the while crying. Wade was startled at first, then felt a warmth he'd never felt before. Before things could go any further, he pushed her back slightly and said,

"There's something I have to explain about myself to you."

"You don't have to explain anything if you don't want to, Wade."

He paused a moment, then answered, "I know you and the others have seen my scars. I want to tell you how I got them."

Taking a deep breath, he began. "After my parents died, and my little brother and sister went with the adoption people, I was left to work out our family debt in a place known as the Sloan stone pits in Boston. I was young, and I made a lot of mistakes while cutting the stones. Every time I made a mistake, I was given lashes by the pit boss – and at eight years old, I made a lot of mistakes. But I learned how to cut and fit stone, and most importantly, I learned how to enjoy the simple things most people don't think of. Like the beauty of a sunrise, or a welcome rain on a hot summer day, or a cool breeze when the air is so thick with dust a boy can hardly breathe."

Linda sat quietly and listened like she had never listened before to his every word.

He continued, "I learned to think happy thoughts when I was so tired that I couldn't walk out of the stone pit back to the slums and just fell asleep in the quarry. I learned to thank God for each day that I could find enough food in the garbage dump so I wouldn't go hungry for days at a time. I would catch rainwater in the hollows of the rocks I had cut, and I thanked God for each drop. I learned that not all people are bad, just some, so I decided a long time ago to always be happy and give of myself to those around me."

He took her hand.

"You see, I only had one thing I could give, and that was love. And I figured that God wanted me to be the very best I could be, so I gave love to my fellow workers, who were bonded slaves, like me. My slavery lasted twelve long, hard years, and at age twenty, with my debt fully paid and my way clear to leave, I began to search for my brother and sister."

"After three years, I found my sister Iris. She lives in Great Falls, Montana, she's married with a child and is a schoolteacher. About a year later, I found my brother; rather, I found his grave. He took sick on the trip to Pennsylvania and died of a fever. So, I came to Texas to escape the northern cold and the dark cold stone pits."

Now he looked into her eyes. "My scars are on my back, but my soul is untouched. And now that you know my past, I have only one question to ask you. Does my having been a bonded slave make any difference to you?"

She smiled through her tears and replied, "You're not a slave anymore, and if you were, it would not matter to me in any way."

He smiled back at her, then said, "I need to talk to James. May I talk to him now?'

She nodded and went to get James, who was still sleeping. The boy stumbled in still half-asleep, until he saw Wade sitting up on the edge of the bed. He ran over, threw his arms around Wade's neck and began to cry, saying, "Thanks God for answering my prayers."

After a moment, Wade asked Linda to go get Doc Buzz while he talked to James man to man. She looked puzzled but honored the request. Once she'd left Wade said, "James, I am going to ask you something, and I want you to tell me straight out. You and I get along well and I don't want to hurt you in any way. But I find myself in love with your mother, and I love you as well.

So, I'm asking you, as man of this house, may I ask your mother to marry me?"

James' lost smile came back bigger than ever. "Yes, Wade, yes! I would be proud to call you 'Pop', if that's all right!"

Wade chuckled and said, "And I'd be proud to call you my son. Do you think your mom will say yes?"

James shrugged his shoulders. "I don't know, all you can do is ask – but I won't say a word, I'll let you decide when to 'pop the question', Pop!"

It was agreed the two men would try for the best time to make the question have the answer they both wanted to hear. But when would be the best time?

Linda returned with Doc Buzz and noticed right off that the two men in her life were up to something. But her woman's instinct told her not to pry. The doctor looked Wade over and said he was healing well, prescribing sunshine and food. Linda promised that he'd get plenty of both.

***

The word spread quickly about Wade's recovery, and people began to come by to speak with and check on him. Every now and again, the question of his scars would come up, mostly from young children. Wade never failed to tell his story about the scars and what he'd learned from his past, and he always gave God the credit for getting him through his young life.

The main part of the courthouse was finished, but Wade and James had more to do. The detailed hand work, the actual art of cutting shapes and designs on the courthouse was their job for three more months. Wade worked hard and James learned fast, and soon, the work was complete.

***

On opening day, the entire county turned out, ladies in their best dresses and men in their Sunday suits, just as it had started. The courthouse would be opened for all to see and admire. As the mayor, Nathan Richard, made his speech and the ribbon cut, the crowd cheered. Wade Gold made his way up the steps to the mayor's side.

The mayor turned to him and said, "Would you like to say a few words?"

"Yes," Wade replied. He faced the crowd and announced, "Linda Wilson, come up here, please."

Linda made her way up the steps to Wade's side, along with young James.

Wade continued, "I want to thank all of you for giving me a chance to build something for man to remember men by. My skill and trade, as you know, was taught to me by my father, and I like to think he had a hand in this building. I lost my dad at an early age, and I know how much a boy needs a father. But I also know how much a man needs his wife. My dad lost his wife and then lost his life. I guess that was the only way he could be with her forever. And being together is what God intended for us to be."

"So, in full view of God and all our friends," he turned to Linda, "Linda Wilson, I am saying I love you, I need you, and will you honor me by being my wife?"

Linda stood motionless for a second, and the crowd was as silent as sleeping lambs. Then Wade bent down on one knee and held up a gold wedding band. Linda flew into Wade's arms as she yelled for all to hear, "Yes, my darling, yes, I'll marry you!"

Wade looked over Linda's shoulder, and got a wink from young James. As the crowd erupted in a loud cheer, Wade realized he was at last truly free.

The first marriage license issued by the clerk in the new courthouse went to Wade Gold and Linda Wilson, two people who came to Wise County alone, and who by the grace of God built a future and a great courthouse.

Elk Hunter

James was his given Christian name, but most everybody called him Jim. And at forty-six, he considered himself to be doing well, although if you asked him, he'd have said he wasn't anything special in the world; he had a house, a job, and he had family that loved him. Then again, he'd also had his share of run-ins with different folks, some whose heads he wound up having to scrape with his knuckles, and he got his eye blackened a couple of times.

As a boy he played sports in school, chased girls, drank a little too much beer sometimes, and of course, never liked to do school work. Really, just a normal life growing up in Texas.

Yes, just your average type man – until one day, when the other Jim was revealed...

Jim had acquired a sixteen-foot long fishing boat, and he used it every chance he got. He liked to drift fish for catfish on Bridgeport Lake during the heat of the day in June, July and August. During that time of year the winds in this part of Texas – Wise County, to be exact – were normally out of the east, and he would maneuver his boat to the middle of the lake, just east of the Boy Scout camp, stop his boat, and let the wind push him back west towards the shore. This method usually netted him three to four catfish weighing anywhere from two pounds all the way up to the size that could and did break his fishing line; he guessed those to weigh in at ten pounds or better, but it was only a guess, seeing as how they got away. He usually fished alone, but he didn't mind. It gave him time to think and time to talk to his Lord.

There was a river that fed into the lake from the north, and he'd heard that it too was pretty good for catching channel cat. On this day, instead of turning into the main body of the lake as he usually did, Jim trawled northwest up the river, looking for a good fishing spot. As he traveled, he noticed that on the right side of the riverbank the rocks along the shore got larger and larger, and soon became a cliff-type shore line. Some of them were fifteen to twenty-five-foot high and flat on top, making a stone wall of sorts.

Jim continued trolling his way upriver for about thirty-five minutes, then started looking around for a good place to cast his line. Going around a wide bend in the river, he found a large swag that he guessed to be about three hundred yards wide, and again the right side of the riverbank was high cliffs. Across on the left bank he could see a fair number of old oak and cedar trees.

At this point in the river he could feel a good southeast breeze that he knew would carry his boat from the tree line toward the cliffs. Jim decided to try this area first, and to him the spot looked perfect – except for one thing. Before, the cliff side of the river had a house every so often, but in this area, there were no houses, no telephone poles or power lines, and no other boats. He shrugged. It really didn't bother him at the time; in fact, he liked the solitude.

He fixed up his rod and reel and began to fish just like always – bait right on the bottom, a hook with fresh shrimp, and a quarter-ounce weight about twelve inches above the hook. He checked his watch and made a mental note that it was June fifteenth, two-thirty-four p.m. He liked to track this so that if the fishing was good, he'd know what time of day to come back on future trips.

He fished, and just as he planned the breeze carried him across the river at just the right speed. He checked his distance from the cliffs occasionally as he didn't want to lose his sense of position and be pushed into them. Jim pulled up his lines about ten feet from the cliffs, boated back across the river, and started the whole process again. But each time he went upriver a bit, to make sure he thoroughly covered the area with his bait.

On his third trip back across the river to restart the pattern, something on the left bank caught his eye. Jim didn't think much of it at the time, knowing the area to be full of wild game. But still, he reasoned, seeing a fox or deer or wolf out in the open would be exciting. So, he started to pay closer attention each time he boated back across.

On his sixth trip across the river he noticed a thumping sound, something he hadn't heard before. He listened for a moment and the sound seemed to fade away as the wind gently pushed him toward the right bank. Then again movement on the left caught his eye. Now, he was forty-six and wore glasses, so he had to make sure that what he thought he saw was in fact what he saw. This time he traveled closer to the tree line area than before, watching the left bank intently.

Suddenly, Jim stopped and motor and drifted in silence toward the bank, keeping his eye on the object that had gotten his attention. The closer he got, the more he couldn't believe his eyes. Oh, he'd seen pictures, of course, but never one in real life, and up this close. He removed his glasses and rubbed his eyes to make sure he wasn't just seeing things.

But sure enough, he was looking at the most beautiful Sioux Indian girl. She was tiny, barely over five feet tall, with long dark hair that reached her waist. But even more eye-catching was her clothing. She was dressed in light brown buckskin, with blue and yellow beadwork down the front and across the shoulders. On her feet he noticed lace-up moccasins which also were adorned with blue and yellow beads forming a star pattern on the front and top.

Jim's boat drifted up next to the shore, and he just sat there for a moment looking at this beautiful person in her costume. Then he noticed the woman was looking directly at him. Both were still for a moment, then the woman smiled.

"Hello," Jim said. "What are you doing out here, dressed like that?"

The Indian woman smiled again, turned, and walked into the trees. Then she stopped and motioned for him to follow. He sat in his boat, watching her, as she motioned again, this time with an even bigger smile.

Jim stood up, climbed over the bow of his boat, then took hold of the rope and dragged the boat onto shore. He tied the boat to a nearby tree, and when he looked up again the woman had walked another fifteen feet into the tree line. He started to follow her when he heard again the strange thumping sound, which seemed to be coming from the direction she was headed.

"Wait," Jim said. "Lady, what's going on? Is this a party or something?"

The woman smiled and laughed a little, then motioned to him again to follow. Jim began to sense that things were not quite right, and maybe he should turn back before he got himself into trouble. But a small voice inside him said, "Go on, this is what you are meant to do. This is a good thing. Don't be afraid, nothing bad will happen."

Jim found himself walked towards the woman, who had stayed and waited for him to catch up. As he approached her, she smiled and reached out her hand. He took her hand in his, and she said, "Come, Elk Hunter, the Council is waiting for you! They wish to hear your words – they need your wisdom."

Elk Hunter? Jim thought. *Who is she calling Elk Hunter?*

Looking down, he noticed he was now wearing buckskin lace-up moccasins and a pair of buckskin chaps. Jim stopped dead in his tracks and examined his entire body; he was now dressed as an Indian brave, loin cloth and all, no shirt, and his hair had changed to shoulder length and coal black. He wore a head band and a large knife in a buckskin sheath at his side. He also noticed a large tooth on a string of rawhide around his neck. It looked like an elk's tooth – it was too big to be from any sort of canine species.

Jim turned around and looked back toward the river, but to his shock the river was gone! He ran back to where he'd left his boat tied up and found nothing – no boat, no motor, no fishing gear. He turned back to the woman, who exclaimed, "What's wrong, my husband? You have a strange look on your face?"

"Where's my boat? Where's the river?"

She laughed and clasped his hand again. "Silly man. No more joking. The Council is waiting. Hunter of Otter sent me to find you!"

The woman led Jim back into the forest and up a small incline, and he noticed the thumping sound he'd heard before was back - and getting louder. When they crested the incline, Jim could neither believe nor understand what he was seeing.

It was an Indian village, with some thirty teepees and sixty to seventy people, all dressed in a similar fashion to the woman beside him. The setting was too real not to be real.

Jim stopped again, but this time held on to her hand. Looking into her eyes, he asked, "What is your name?"

Her smile faded into confusion. "What's my name? What's wrong with you, Elk Hunter?"

Jim replied, "I don't know, but I am going to find out. Now, what is your name?"

Her confusion turned to irritation, and she pulled her hand away and snapped, "Elk Hunter, we have been as one for three summers now, and if you don't know that my name is Blue Bird in Wind you are in bad trouble!"

Bad trouble. She might be right, he mused, before telling her, "I'm just joking with you, my little Blue Bird in Wind. Why did you come and get me?"

She rolled her eyes. "I told you, the Council is waiting to hear your words. Hunter of Otter sent me after you."

"Hunter of Otter? Who is he?"

"Now you don't know your own father-in-law, the Chief of our village?"

Again, Jim responded, "Just kidding, just kidding."

Her eyes blazed. "You better get down to Council meeting and stop playing like small boy, Elk Hunter, before I get medicine man and tell him you have lost your mind."

Jim walked in the direction she was pointing, while she continued to yell at him. "Yep, she's a wife all right," he muttered under his breath, still trying to make sense of it all. He figured he would go to this Council meeting, and maybe someone there would be able to help him find the river, his boat, and his clothes.

It was then he realized that the chaps he was wearing had no back to them. There he was, walking around among people he did not know – including women and children – almost buck naked. *Well, more like* butt *naked, hah, hah,* his inner clown thought. The whole thing made him extremely uncomfortable. But right now, he had more important things to find out, and maybe the Council could help.

As he made his way to the Council tent, he noticed several things about the village. He saw older women working at tanning ranks while younger women hung meat strips on drying racks. Children of all ages ran about laughing and playing. But he noticed one thing that puzzled him most of all. Everyone he passed, young and old alike, called out "Elk Hunter", in almost a reverent tone.

What he couldn't understand was why.

Jim reached the Council tent and realized that was where the thumping sound was coming from. As he entered, he found ten to twelve men inside, three of whom were seated to his left and beating on drums. As soon as he walked in, the drums stopped and several of the younger men rose to their feet.

He remembered what Blue Bird in Wind had told him, and asked, "Where is Hunter of Otter?"

And as his eyes adjusted to the darkness, he heard a voice beckon. "I am here, my son; come and sit and smoke with me." Looking across the tent, he could see the man who had spoken. The man was dressed in full buckskin clothing and wore a head band with many beads. Jim guessed him to be in his sixties, and he had a strong appearance of leadership about his manner.

As his made his way over to Hunter of Otter, others he passed in the tent called out, "Elk Hunter". He took his seat beside the old man and said nothing as Hunter of Otter removed a long-stemmed pipe from a leather sleeve, then packed the bowl of the pipe with what Jim thought might be grass and horse droppings.

The warrior took a small twig from the fire and held it to the bowl as he began to puff on the pipe. Soon the mixture took hold and smoke came out of the end into Hunter of Otter's mouth. He took a couple of long puffs, then blew the smoke upwards toward the hole in the top of the rent. Hunter of Otter then passed the pipe to Jim and smiled widely. Jim could see that the old man had very good teeth and a wide flat nose, with brown eyes and high cheekbones. Nodding and smiling back, Jim took the pipe, and began to inhale the smoke.

Now, Jim was a smoker; in fact, he smoked about two packs of cigarettes a day, so he figured this would be no problem. Suddenly the taste and smell hit him, and all at once he began to cough and felt like he was going to throw up. But he was able to control his coughing and blew what smoke was left towards the roof of the tent as he'd seen Hunter of Otter do.

Jim took another puff or two, just to show the rest he could handle this terrible blend, then offered the pipe back to Hunter of Otter. The expression on the warrior's face let him know quickly that move was incorrect, so Jim turned and passed the pipe to the man seated on the other side of him. Hunter of Otter smiled again and nodded his approval, and the drummers began to play once more, but this time they also began to chant as well.

Jim listened to the rhythms and moved his foot to the music. Then he noticed that Hunter of Otter had leaned back on a pile of animal skins and seemed to be in deep thought. Turning slightly, he saw a pile behind him as well, so he mirrored the warrior's movement. Casting his gaze around the tent he confirmed each man, after taking his turn with the pipe, was reclining, as if to think things out.

After fifteen to twenty minutes, Hunter of Otter sat upright again, and asked, "I am glad Blue Bird in Wind found you. Were you thinking on our problem, my son?"

Jim had no idea what the man was talking about, and figured the less he said, the better, until he could figure out exactly what was going on. So, he kept his answer vague. "Yes," he replied to Hunter of Otter, "I've been walking and thinking this matter over, but I would hear the Council's thoughts before I make up my mind." And he thought to himself, *Smooth, dodged that one.*

But the old warrior admonished, "My son, we have talked on the matter and have been waiting to hear your voice!"

Jim felt trapped and knew he'd better think fast. Suddenly he heard himself say, "This is true, my Chief, but I have not heard the Council's words, and will do so now."

Hunter of Otter stared at Jim intently for a long moment, then answered, "Very well, my son, I feel you are wise to hear the older ones' thoughts on this matter."

The man to whom Jim had passed the pipe sat up and announced, "I am Dog that Howls, and I think we must not let this go; we must act, and soon. That is my voice."

The next man spoke. "I am Flying Crow, and I will say this. Time is important on this matter. What we do must be done soon."

At this point Jim still had no clue what the topic of discussion was and felt at this rate he'd never find out. He did his best to not show his impatience as the conversation continued around the tent.

"I, Running Horse, say we must be sure of our actions and be ready to face them as braves."

To Running Horse's left, another man leaned forward. "Important matters such as this must be considered very wisely. We don't want to make any mistakes. That's what I, Blanket Maker, think!"

Great, Jim groaned to himself. *Four men speak and still no further along as what the hell is going on.*

And there were only two of them left to speak – Hunter of Otter, and an even older man who had sat quietly during all the other declarations.

A long silence, then Hunter of Otter, spoke to the man. "Dear Friend, please give us the wisdom of your years and knowledge on this matter."

Again, a long silence, and finally the old man sat up, and began to speak. "I, Moon on Rise, have had a troubled heart over this matter, for I have seen visions of this long before now." He paused for a time, then resumed.

"My dreams have puzzled me. Sometimes being a medicine man and spirit leader is very hard. The Great Spirit talks to me when he wants to and tells me what

He thinks I need to know, nothing else. This time He has said that a young man will come to us from beyond the tomorrows and help us."

A soft murmur from the others listening rippled gently through the pause he took.

"He also told me he would come by water in a canoe with very fast paddles on it. But I do not know what He meant by 'comes from beyond the tomorrows', and I have never before seen a canoe like I was shown." Moon on Rise chuckled softly. "Maybe I am too old to understand my dreams anymore. But I say this, the Great Spirit will send someone. Maybe he already has!" With that, he reclined once again, and fell silent.

Jim now knew his being there did have purpose, and he knew he'd see this adventure through to its end. He had been told by both his mother and father of Indian background on both sides of the family. He'd heard stories of the Great Spirit, or Great White Light, ever since he was a child, and now, having stepped into a setting like none other he'd ever seen, he was determined not to let whatever God had planned for his life get away.

All in attendance at the Council sat in silence after the talk given by Moon on Rise. Jim knew he was the one spoken of in the old man's vision and now he knew he must find out the exact problem and find the answer, no matter what the problem was. After all, these people had already shown him great respect, by the way he'd been greeted as he passed through the village.

Jim leaned forward and studied the fire, watching the flames, noticing how the coals were glowing; it seemed to be talking to him. He began to pray, at first to himself, then out loud. He could hear the tom toms in the background, and the song the young braves were chanting.

He heard himself say, "Great Father of our land, of our people, we need You to show the answer and to guide us; we need Your knowledge so may handle this matter the way You would have us handle it. We ask You, Great One, to show a vision, a sign, and give us Your answer!"

Silence resumed in the teepee once more, and all sat looking into the fire. After a few minutes of quiet, Hunter of Otter sat up, placing his hand on Jim's shoulder. Hunter of Otter had not spoken yet, and Jim knew he was the last hope of finding out more specifics as to the problem being considered.

Hunter of Otter remained quiet a time longer, his hand still on Jim's shoulder. Then finally the warrior said, "I, Chief of this village, Hunter of Otter, must say what I feel. My son by my daughter's marriage, Elk Hunter, is a brave man as we all know. He has faced our enemies many times and has always brought us honor. He has shown much wisdom tonight by asking for the Council Fathers to speak before he makes his decision. I know that his prayer to the Great Spirit will be answered and I feel that to ask him to make the final decision on our talked before he receives the answer from the Great Spirit would be foolish."

Jim looked at him and reminded, "But Hunter of Otter, I have also not yet heard your voice on this matter."

As he watched the flames of fire dance, the old man replied, "All here know my feelings about the ones that have been taken from us, but I am no longer strong enough for battles. I must now be wise enough to let our strongest brave have time to work out a plan. I must let Elk Hunter have time to decide."

Upon hearing Hunter of Otter's words, Jim rose and walked around to the teepee's entrance. He turned, looked back at the Chief and the medicine man, and announced, "I will sleep and dream. Tonight, the Great Spirit will reveal to me the plan I need." Then he stepped outside.

His first thought as he saw the sunset was of his wife Belinda. He didn't want her to be worried, but if he couldn't find the river, much less his boat, how could he tell her where he was? No. He would have to play this out and worry about the world he'd left behind later.

A voice called out. "Elk Hunter."

Looking up, Jim saw Blue Bird in Wind standing by a teepee. "Come, my husband," she beckoned. "Your food is cooked and ready to eat!"

He walked over and sat down by the fire, and Blue Bird in Wind handed him a bowl of what looked like stew. Jim remembered that in Indian culture, forks and spoons did not exist, so he began to eat with his fingers, and was surprised to find it felt very natural to him, as if he'd been eating this way his whole life. Blue Bird dipped some stew out for herself, and as she sat beside him, she asked, "What did the Council decide?"

"They are going to let me be the one who decides what to do."

"Take your time," she told him. "The Council has made a wise choice. Since you were with the others when they were taken, you will know best how to get them back!"

Jim sat quietly, eating, not noticing how good the food was, or even that Blue Bird in Wind had gone inside the teepee, because his mind was busy reviewing the clues he had to work with. He thought of the day's events, and the strange happenings that had occurred. He knew he was to do something – but what? Again, he watched the fire. Soon darkness was all around him, and still no answers to his hundreds of questions. Finally, he realized the best thing to do was recap, and try to make the puzzle fit together somehow.

Let's see, he mused. *First, I was fishing; then I met an Indian woman who said I'm her husband; I lost my boat AND the river while following her to an Indian village, where I was honored by everyone and called Elk Hunter; met a chief, a medicine man, and the Council Fathers; and I am supposed to get back some people this Elk Hunter person was with who were taken. I must find a way to get the lost people back and get myself back to the river and my boat. Now, that wasn't too hard to figure out. Right?*

"Yeah, right," he muttered softly to himself.

What he knew for sure was he needed help. He couldn't tell these people who he really was, or where he'd come from – they would think he'd gone mad. But he needed help. He needed to know where the lost people were lost, how many of them, and – wait a minute! There *was* help here, right under his very nose. There was one person in the village who would not think him crazy and who could and would answer all his questions.

It would be an interesting conversation, to be sure, but Jim felt it was his only chance of solving anything. He would go and talk to this man, alone. He knew this man would understand him being from another time, another world; after all, Moon on Rise had told of such in the Council meeting.

"Need to talk to the medicine man," he whispered. He looked around, startled to see Blue Bird in Wind was no longer seated next to him. He called to her, and when she came outside, he said, "Take me to the medicine man."

She looked confused at this, and replied, "Take you, my husband? Have you forgotten which teepee is Moon on Rise?"

Jim rose to his feet and looked into her eyes. "I do not expect you to understand, wife, but ever since the others were taken my life has been touched by the Great Spirit; please just do as I have asked!"

She leaned down, took a piece of wood from the fire, and holding it out like a torch led the way toward the center of the village. They'd walked about thirty yards when she stopped and pointed to a teepee to the right about ten yards away.

"Thank you, Blue Bird in Wind," he told her. "Now, return, and do not wait up for me. This will be a long night."

As she turned to walk back to their teepee, he heard her mutter, "Ask Moon on Rise for medicine to restore your memory, my husband."

Jim chuckled at that. *Blue Bird in Wind is a lot like my wife back in my world; Belinda's told me pretty much the same thing!* he realized.

Now he called out. "Moon on Rise, it is I, Elk Hunter. I need to talk with you."

After a moment the teepee flap opened, and a voice replied, "Enter, Elk Hunter, and welcome."

Jim entered, and began to speak. "Moon on Rise, the Great Spirit has spoken to me and I came to you for help." He noticed that the man had gone from half-asleep to wide awake, and Jim knew he had his full attention. Jim felt it best to be honest, but also take it slowly.

"Moon on Rise, I respect your dreams and visions, and what I am going to tell you, you must believe and not fear. The Great Spirit has indeed sent you a helper from beyond the tomorrows. Is it I."

He paused, waiting for the old man to respond, but Moon on Rise just looked intently at him and did not speak. Jim cleared his throat and continued.

"I may look like Elk Hunter, but I am not him; my real name is Jim, and I came to you and your village to help your people. I did not know why I was brought here at first. But now I think it was to help bring back those that were taken. Moon on Rise, do you believe me?"

Moon on Rise tilted his head slightly, and asked, "What sort of name is 'Jim'? What does it mean?"

Jim thought for a moment, then answered, "It means One Who Finds Lost People."

The old man nodded. "If you are the one the Spirit showed me in my dream, where is your canoe with many paddles?"

"When I came from my world to yours, I had to leave it at the bank of the river."

Moon on Rise leaned forward with excitement. "Will you show it to me?"

Jim knew the medicine man would not believe him if he could not produce his boat. "I cannot take you to my boat; to do so, you would have to leave this world and travel into the world of beyond tomorrows. I can draw you a picture of it. You said you had seen it in your dream, didn't you?"

Moon on Rise nodded in affirmation, reached over to his right and produced a clean animal skin, a quill and some sort of dye. He handed the items to Jim, saying, "Make me a picture. If it is what I saw in my dream, then I will believe you and will answer all your questions."

Jim wasn't an artist – not even close – but when he took the quill in hand and dipped it into the dye, he felt he could manage a picture of his own boat. Leaning over the skin, he very carefully began to draw. Again and again, he dipped the quill into the dye. He first drew the body of the boat, then using a side view, added the motor. For some reason he felt compelled to make the propeller stand out.

Pulling away from the finished drawing, Jim watched the medicine man's face carefully as Moon on Rise leaned over and inspected the picture. The old man looked at it for a long time, and then asked, "What color is this canoe?"

"It is like the sky on a clear day," Jim said. "It is blue."

Moon on Rise's eyes were wide, and he sat motionless. Jim, sensing his fear, assured him, "I am not here to hurt anyone. I am here to help you. The Great Spirit has sent me, but you must answer my questions about those who were taken so I can find them and return them safely to this village."

Moon on Rise began to chant and pray as he rose and walked around inside the teepee. He first picked up a rattle made from an old gourd, then reached into a leather bag and threw some powder into the air. This went on for several minutes, then he sat down again. "What is it you need to know, Spirit?"

Jim started to tell him that he was not a spirit, then thought better of it. If he wanted to think Jim a spirit, let him; all Jim wanted was answers.

"I need to know the names of the ones who are missing, and I need to be taken to where they were last seen. Will you take me, Moon on Rise?"

"Yes, at first light," came the reply.

Jim heaved a sigh of relief, and as he left said, "First light then. Sleep well, my old friend."

As he walked back to his teepee, Jim wrestled with how to get the people back; he had a pretty good idea of what had happened but would find out for sure in the morning. And as he got closer to where Blue Bird in Wind waited, he knew that like most women she would probably have questions for him he could not answer.

He slowed his pace as he realized that he'd not only have to dodge questions, but also avoid having to act as a married man with Blue Bird in Wind. He had a wife he loved dearly, and he wanted to avoid trouble at all costs.

Then Jim had an idea. He picked up a stick roughly three feet in length and walked into the teepee. Standing up very straight he thundered, "Woman!" and struck the ground hard with the stick.

Blue Bird in Wind curled into a ball under her buffalo robe. "What is wrong, my husband, what I have done?"

"You know what it is! You have caused eyes in our village to look upon me with laughter; you've been telling the other women in the village about us, haven't you?"

She looked up at him sheepishly then began to lift the robe. He saw a flash of nakedness and began to panic. Then a voice inside him said, "Be firm, be firm."

With a blank expression, he told her, "No, no, that will not work this time. This time I am really mad with you. We have all this trouble in our village, and you and your mouth add to my worries. Now go to sleep. I must walk and think how to solve this problem!"

She tucked the robe back down around herself. He turned on his heel and left the teepee, relieved he'd managed to hold her off for now.

As Jim stood outside the teepee, he refocused his mind to the bigger problem. He knew he had to listen to the old man's words very carefully so he could pick up on small details that would help solve the puzzle. But right now, he needed sleep so his full attention and strength would be best used come the morning light.

Walking away from the teepee he found several buffalo skins and took them with him to the incline where'd he first seen the camp; here he would spend the night and here he'd begin his search in the morning for the lost people. It didn't take long for sleep to overtake him.

***

Just after first light Jim was awakened by the voice of the medicine man calling to him. "Elk Hunter! Elk Hunter, it is I, Moon on Rise. Come, and I will take you to the last footprints of Morning Fawn and Night Dove."

As they walked, Jim asked, "Moon on Rise, how many people were lost?"

"Three," came the reply. "My granddaughters Morning Fawn and Night Dove, and you, Elk Hunter."

Stopping next to the trees where Jim had first taken Blue Bird in Wind's hand, the medicine man pointed to three sets of footprints – one adult-sized, the other two sets much smaller. Jim noticed that the prints were all facing the same direction, into the trees, and were close together. He also noticed that the trees in this area were very tall and were leaning away from the village; the grass was about knee-high, and it too leaned toward the center of the forest, away from the village.

Jim left Moon on Rise's side and walked forward a few steps, then turned and said, "Please, old friend, return to the village. I'll try to find your grandchildren, but I must go alone."

Moon on Rise smiled and said, "I'll be waiting for you, Spirit, and my grandchildren, in my teepee!" Then he turned and walked back up to and over the incline out of Jim's sight.

Jim turned, checking both his direction and that of the footprints. He could tell the prints were made while walking; the toe prints were deeper than the heel prints, which in moccasins would show more readily than in the modern shoe. It was as if the three were walking and talking, then crossed over an invisible line at the same time, taking one step from their world into the world Jim had come from.

He looked again at the trees and grass, and noted that just before the prints stopped, the grass and trees grew straight. He began to walk northward, keeping the bent trees and grass to his left and the straight grass and trees to his right.

Jim walked for hours following this method. As he walked, he realized the wind seemed to be nonexistent where the grass and trees came together, but by watching the tree tops on both sides of this line, he confirmed that they were indeed swaying in the wind. The trees to his right, the ones standing upright, were being blown to his right, while the tops of the leaning tress were being blown to his left, in the direction they were leaning. He could make no logical sense of this.

The late afternoon sun confirmed he'd been walking for about eight hours, and he was hungry and tired, but he'd still found no sign of the missing children or the brave Elk Hunter. He stopped, and was about to turn back when he heard, "Elk Hunter, Elk Hunter, have you found our children?" It was Hunter of Otter.

"No, not yet," Jim replied wearily, then started. How did Hunter of Otter find him? He'd been walking for hours...

Then, just ahead, Jim saw it. Could it be? Yes, the footprints of the missing trio... But wait. These were the prints he'd seen earlier in the day. He'd followed the leaning grass and trees for eight hours and ended up back at the same place he'd begun.

"Wow," he exclaimed. Then it hit him – He'd always kept the leaning trees to his left. He realized he must have walked in a very large circle, yes, that's it! A very large circle, and the trees were leaning *toward the center* of that circle. That had to be the answer. Tomorrow, he'd have to break through the invisible line by walking towards the center of it. He tried to figure out why the trees were leaning, but soon realized it was no use; he would know soon enough, as soon as he crossed over that line into the yet to be tomorrows.

It was late when Jim returned to his teepee and faced Blue Bird in Wind, but he knew he'd have no problem with this woman tonight because of his physical condition. He was tired, in fact so tired that he did not even eat. He entered the teepee, laid down on some animal skins, and went right to sleep.

***

The next morning Jim woke and found his legs were hurting mightily from the previous day's activity. He got to his feet and went outside. The sun was just coming up, and Blue Bird in Wind handed him a bowl of food, saying, "My husband goes to look for lost children again?"

"Yes, Blue Bird in Wind," he replied. "And what is this I am eating? It's good."

The woman smiled. "Same as the other night, my husband – dog!"

Dog. That must be the Indian word for beef, his mind mused, and he shrugged. He was so hungry it didn't matter.

After he ate, he walked up the incline and this time viewed the forest area. He could see the tree line in the distance and now noticed a very large area that did in fact form a circular pattern in what seemed to be the middle of the forest. This is where he hoped to find the children, Elk Hunter, and maybe, his way home.

Home. Jim was sure that by now his family, his wife Belinda and his children, were worried sick. He must solve this problem and get back. Being among these people and remembering his own world, he had learned something about worry – especially worry about someone you loved; it was like a bad toothache. You live with it but don't like it. But with God's help, he'd soon put an end to all the worrying, about Morning Fawn and Night Dove and although the village didn't know it yet, Elk Hunter as well.

He made his way back to the edge of the circle. For some reason, he felt the key to traveling into the circle and finding the lost trio were the last things they'd left behind – their footprints.

Jim carefully examined the prints again, this time studying them closely, taking in every detail. He noticed that on the left front of one of the children's prints was a line about a half-inch long; this might have been from a string or tear in the moccasin. But still, it would identify the child as one who came from the Indian village.

As Jim looked into the forest, he remembered the Lord's Prayer, and the part about walking:

"...Through the valley of the shadow of Death, I will fear no evil, for Thou art with me."

Jim, stepping forward, said aloud, "Amen, Lord, Amen."

About four steps inside the circle he looked back. He could see the prints left by the trio, but noticed he was not leaving any. He now had to devise a way to find this exit point again. He wouldn't be able to retrace his steps – there weren't any. So, he began to break small limbs off the trees as he walked, checking backwards from time to time to make sure he was leaving an identifiable trail.

He'd walked about fifty yards, breaking branches, when he felt a cool wet breeze. It was hitting him in the face, so he walked straight ahead. Suddenly, the breeze stopped. Jim walked another ten feet and felt heat as he passed between two very large oak trees. There it was, the hot summertime he'd left, and he saw his boat and motor still tied to a tree. Once again, he was back in his world. Now he knew how to get home again. But first, he must return to the circle and find the lost ones.

Jim retraced his steps leading back between the large oak trees and stepped back into the circle. He found the branches he'd broken off and knew that now he must listen and watch for any sign of the trio. He knew where he had entered the area, and where he'd exited and found his boat, and guessed that he had covered roughly one-fifth of the circle. It was a like a big pie, and the straight walk he'd taken had only cut off one end of it. He'd have to go back about halfway, then turn left and walk straight. This pattern would cut the remainder of the search area in half and hopefully speed up finding the trio.

As he moved, he noticed the air in the forest was much cooler than both his world and in the Indian village. He'd also noticed that when he'd found his boat, his modern-day clothing had come back as well, but now being back in the forest he was once again dressed like Elk Hunter. This might help him to find the children, who would think he was Elk Hunter, and come to him. But what would he do when and if he found the brave he looked like?

He walked for fifteen minutes, breaking branches as he went, and calling out, "Night Dove, Morning Fawn, where are you? Your grandfather Moon on Rise has sent me to find you!"

He heard no reply.

Jim repeated this for four hours, breaking branches and calling out as he walked. Suddenly there was a rustling sound in the brush just ahead. Being very still and listening very hard, he could hear a small cry, that of a child.

He called out to the children again, and about ten yards in front of him two small girls appeared, one about five years old, the other six. Both were dressed like the other children he'd seen in the village. They began to smile, and ran to Jim with open arms, crying, "Elk Hunter, Elk Hunter, we thought you were dead! Oh, Elk Hunter, take us home please!"

He leaned down, hugged them very tightly, and began to cry.

Morning Fawn asked, "Why do you cry, Elk Hunter? Braves are not supposed to cry!"

Jim looked at them and said, "I cry for happiness, because I've found those I thought were lost; the spirits have blessed us all. Now, why did you say you thought I was dead?"

Night Dove answered, "When you fell and did not move. You hurt your head, there was blood. We thought you were dead."

Jim knew he must take a chance and see if the children could show him the place where the brave had fallen. Thinking quickly, he told him, "You know, when I fell, I lost something, and I've got to get it back before we go home. But I don't remember where I fell. Can you show me?"

Both girls pointed to an area about fifty yards away. "Over there," they said in union.

Taking each child by the hand, Jim walked towards the spot the girls had indicated. He stopped about twenty feet short and urged, "Stay right here, and don't move from this spot, okay?"

Walking over, Jim found himself looking over a drop-off of roughly fifteen feet, and at the bottom he could see the Indian brave, Elk Hunter. He could see the warrior's chest moving, so Elk Hunter had not died, but did need medical help.

Returning to the children, Jim said, "Let's go home."

Night Dove asked, "Did you find what you had lost, Elk Hunter?"

Jim said, "No, maybe I will find it on the way home!"

As they walked, he asked the children how they'd made it through two nights. They told of holding each other at night and singing songs their mother had taught them, and of eating berries during the day, but most of all they told of hiding until someone came to take them home.

Approaching the exit, Jim was glad he'd been a Boy Scout and knew how to mark a trail; this made the return to the village a lot easier. When he reached the trail where he'd first walked through one end of the circle, he turned left to go to the village. Jim stopped and picked up the children and told them, "I will not lose you this time, my pretty ones." The children, tired and hungry, laughed and wrapped their arms around his neck.

Following the marked trail, Jim walked until he found the exit point and could see the footprints just ahead. In his mind, there was a slight fear that crossing over into the Indian world would somehow change him again, but his fears were put to rest as he heard a voice say, "Return the children to the village; all will be alright."

Taking a deep breath, Jim stepped into the very spot where the children had last been seen. To his delight, nothing happened except the temperature change of about ten degrees.

He made his way up the incline carrying the children and as they reached the top, he gave out a great cheer. He carried them all the way to the center of the village and gave them to their grandfather Moon on Rise, who by this time had big tears in his eyes.

The old man exclaimed, "Thank you, Elk Hunter, the Great Spirit as blessed all of us this day with the return of our children!"

The two children were covered by women smiling and crying. Jim heard cries of "Mommy! Mommy!" from the children, and it was truly as happy a reunion as he'd ever witnessed.

After a few minutes, he took Moon on Rise to one side away from the crowd and told of finding the true Elk Hunter. "I will need you and Hunter of Otter to with me into the circle to help bring Elk Hunter back," he told the medicine man, then explained how he'd marked the trail and that Elk Hunter had been injured by a fall, striking his head on a stone.

The old man thought for a moment, then answered, "We must tell Hunter of Otter the truth of this matter, and we must reveal the truth about you."

Jim didn't know if that was going to be the smartest thing to do, but now knowing the way back, he could escape if he had to. So, he followed Moon on Rise to Hunter of Otter's teepee.

As the three men sat inside talking Jim watched Hunter of Otter's face as Moon on Rise explained about Jim and the dreams of the canoe with many paddles. Moon on Rise showed the picture Jim had drawn to the village chief, told him Jim's real name, then concluded, "Hunter of Otter, this name means "Finder of Lost People', and this man you see in the body of Elk Hunter is a Spirit."

All was quiet for a moment, then the Chief replied, "Welcome, Spirit."

Jim said, "Thank you, Hunter of Otter. Now I need your help. When I found the children, I also found Elk Hunter, but he is hurt, and I need help in bringing him back so he can get the medicine man's powerful medicine to get well. Will you help Moon on Rise and me?"

Hunter of Otter accepted the challenge and now looked at Jim in a different way. The three men talked more on the matter, then made plans to rescue Elk Hunter. Moon on Rise would go to his teepee and get the herbs and potions he would need for Elk Hunter's injury, and Hunter of Otter would summon two more braves to help. They agreed to meet at the top of the incline in a short while.

Jim went to check on Night Dove and Morning Fawn, since he felt he might not see them again. He found both children had been fed and were sleeping soundly in their mother's arms. As he watched them, he smiled, thinking of his own children at that age, and he was very proud of being part of their rescue.

He traveled to the top of the incline and was soon joined by Hunter of Otter and two other braves – Mule Deer, and Little Bear, who both greeted him with,

"Welcome, Spirit, welcome." Hunter of Otter explained that he'd told them about Jim and his reason for being among the people. Jim now knew that by the time they returned, the entire village would know exactly who he was and why he had come.

As soon as Moon on Rise joined the group Jim led them to the entry point. He paused, saying, "We have about a four-hour walk, and must hurry; Moon on Rise had medicine that will make Elk Hunter better. One thing. All of you must stay with me, and not the leave the trail I have marked; you must always stay where you can see me. Do you understand?"

All in the group replied, "Yes, Spirit."

Jim turned, walked into the circle, and found the broken branches from his first trip. As he moved forward, he checked over his shoulder from time to time and always saw the four other men well within sight. After about two hours, he stopped and sat on the ground, with the others gathered around him.

"Why we did stop?" Moon on Rise asked.

"To let my friend Moon on Rise rest!" Jim answered.

Moon on Rise scowled. "My years are many, but my heart is strong!"

Jim smiled at him and replied, "I know, my friend, but when we get to Elk Hunter you must be able to give him your medicine. Without you, we will lose the brave."

A few minutes later the group started off again. The remaining two hours moved quickly, and Jim once again found the clearing where Elk Hunter lay. Walking to the edge of the drop-off once more, he watched to see if Elk Hunter was still breathing. He could clearly see the brave was indeed breathing and, in fact, looked stronger than before.

Little Bear and Mule Deer had brought rawhide ropes with them. They tied them to trees then threw them over the edge of the drop-off so the party could climb down to Elk Hunter. Once they reached his side, Moon on Rise began to administer his medicine. Meanwhile Little Bear, Mule Deer, and Hunter of Otter were making a litter to carry Elk Hunter on.

Jim asked, "Do you think Elk Hunter will be all right?"

Moon on Rise nodded. "Yes. My medicine is strong, and the brave is strong. Together, the strength of Elk Hunter and my medicine will work."

After Moon on Rise made a solution of herbs and water, he held Elk Hunter's head up and poured the mixture down the injured man's throat. The brave drank but was very still. As the litter neared completion, Elk Hunter began to move a little and moan. Jim looked at Moon on Rise, and the two men smiled at the same time.

The rescue team placed Elk Hunter on the litter, with Little Bear, Mule Deer, and Hunter of Otter pulling on the ropes as Jim and Moon on Rise pushed, and they were able to bring Elk Hunter along and climb out of the drop-off.

As they made their way back to the exit point, the braves asked Jim many questions about the world they called Beyond Tomorrow. He tried to explain as best he could about his world and how it was, but he could tell from his talking that the braves were glad they did not live there.

When they reached the exit point, Jim noticed Moon on Rise was exhausted. Knowing the temperature would be hotter outside the circle, Jim announced, "We must stop here and wait a few minutes!" Placing the litter on the ground, the party rested.

Then Little Bear cried, "Look! Our Elk Hunter has returned, the medicine has worked!"

Everyone looked and saw Elk Hunter had opened his eyes, and the first question he asked was, "How are the children? Are they all right?"

Hunter of Otter leaned over and reassured him. 'Yes, my son, they are all right. They are with their mother."

Then Elk Hunter noticed Jim, and asked, "Who is this person who looks like me?"

Moon on Rise answered, saying, "He is a Spirit!"

"A spirit! Am I dead?" Elk Hunter looked confused.

Moon on Rise and the others laughed a little, and the medicine man told him, "No, you're not dead. We will explain as we carry you home."

Picking up the litter, they continued toward the village, with Hunter of Otter telling Elk Hunter the story of Jim the Spirit who had come to help find the children. As they carried Elk Hunter and he listened to the Chief's words, he watched Jim, and Jim could tell Elk Hunter had lots of questions on his mind. Jim knew that he'd answer Elk Hunter's and the rest of the village's questions, but first they needed to get Elk Hunter safely back to his village and his teepee.

As they exited the circle and walked up the incline, Jim began to feel very strange. At first, he thought it was because of the heat, so he didn't pay much attention. When they reached the top of the incline and started down the other side toward the village, they heard the cries of joy coming from the people. As they carried the litter, the people called out each of their names, but not Jim's name; in fact, now the people seemed to be afraid of him. This made Jim feel even worse than earlier.

Then Jim realized what was happening. These people were seeing, for the first time, *two* Elk Hunters, not just the one they had known for so long. He could understand their difficulty in handling this matter.

Once they reached Elk Hunter's teepee and he was taken inside, the Chief called a meeting of the entire village. It took some doing, but after Hunter of Otter and Moon on Rise explained to the people and answered their questions, the people began to understand why and what had brought Jim to their midst and began to accept his presence among them.

Jim did not himself understand all that had happened, or how. But he wanted one person to explain how she found him.

He went to see Blue Bird in Wind and talked to her about their first meeting. At first, she thought he was talking about the time that she and her husband Elk Hunter had met. But soon he was able to explain he was talking about only two days prior.

She said, "The day Hunter of Otter sent me to find you, the children had only been missing for a few hours and I found you just below the incline."

Jim knew now that when he touched Blue Bird in Wind's hand on that first day, that was their first meeting. It was not her he'd seen at the river bank; it was not her that had motioned to him to follow. Although it looked like her, it was not the same person, because Blue Bird in Wind – or at least *this* Blue Bird in Wind – knew nothing of the river, or of seeing Jim's boat, or of beckoning to him. The only memory she had was her husband coming up to her and taking her hand.

Jim's question now was, who was it he'd seen that day on the river bank? Who was it that had gotten him to follow? Then he remembered he'd lost sight of the woman on that first day, but just for a moment; in fact, just at the same spot the exit was now, where the footprints had been found.

After talking to Blue Bird in Wind, Jim went to see Elk Hunter, who by now was sitting up and feeling better. As Jim approached, he said, "Elk Hunter, it is I, Jim. May I talk to you?"

Elk Hunter smiled, saying, "Welcome, Spirit, you honor me by coming."

The two sat and talked, but the only thing Elk Hunter could tell Jim was that he and the children had gotten lost in what he called 'the cool forest'.

Jim thanked the warrior for his words, then left to go say good-bye to the people. Something told him it was time to leave and be with his own world again.

It was getting late when Jim reached the top of the incline and turned to wave his last goodbye to the people. He could see Hunter of Otter, Moon on Rise, Little Bear, Mule and Night Dove, as well as Morning Fawn, and he saw Blue Bird in Wind and Elk Hunter standing hand in hand in front of their teepee. He heard them call out as he moved down the other side toward the forest, "We'll not forget you, Jim, Spirit, Finder of Lost People; we will not forget what you did!"

Smiling, Jim once again entered the forest circle and followed the broken branches to the two large oak trees. Just beyond, he could see his boat and the river, and he figured he had just enough daylight left to make it back to the boat dock and load up for home.

He reached the tree and had started to untie his boat when he felt a cool breeze and then a hand on his shoulder. Jim turned around and saw the woman who looked like Blue Bird in Wind, but he knew it was not her.

The two stood for a moment in silence, then the woman spoke.

"James, this you have done is good; you let us use you to find the children and rescue the brave, and you never faltered in any way. Please never lose the faith that you have now, the faith that your forefathers have given you, and remember that this world is not your final home. My world is waiting for you and you will be welcomed."

He answered, "I guess I'll never understand all of this, but I want to thank you and whoever for this adventure. Maybe God will bless me someday and I will see you again."

She smiled, and before she walked back to the two oak trees said, "He has already blessed you. Go now, with that blessing." And just as she had appeared the first time, in the twinkle of an eye, she was gone.

Jim pushed his boat away from the bank and tried to start the engine. To his surprise, it started on the first attempt; usually after sitting a few days, the old motor was hard to start, but not this time. That's when he noticed he was back in his regular clothes.

He put the motor in reverse, and after getting a distance from the bank, let the boat swing around and eased it into forward gear. He headed back down the river, watching the shore line all the while. About a hundred years downriver from the two oak trees, he felt a cool breeze on the water, and just for a moment he could hear the tom toms of the braves and their high-pitched chant of all the yesterdays already gone.

The boat trip back to the loading ramp took about thirty-five minutes, and as Jim was loading his boat, he recognized a couple of older men fishing next to the ramp – the same men he'd seen two days earlier.

"I see you gentlemen are back again," he called to them.

One of them responded, "What do you mean, back again?"

"Well, didn't I see you guys there two days ago?" Jim asked, confused.

The second man chimed in with, "Two days ago it rained. No, you saw us about four hours ago. Don't you remember? Boy, you must have been out in this sun all day long."

Jim hurriedly checked his watch, the one his wife had given him for Christmas. Sure enough, it read six-forty-three p.m., June fifteenth.

He stood, dumbfounded, before he gathered himself enough to say softly, "Wow. What a fishing trip!"

As he was putting the boat on the trailer, he noticed his reflection in the water. There it was, around his neck, the rawhide with an elk tooth. He tied his boat to the trailer, then climbed into the truck for the drive home. That's when he found the small child's moccasin lying on the seat of his pickup. He turned it over and saw a small half-inch tear in the toe.

Blessed, yes, blessed by the spirit world of days gone, present, and yet to come....

So– If you're ever out on Bridgeport Lake during the heat of the summer months, in the afternoon, and you come across a blue boat tied to a tree, well, maybe Jim is just visiting some old friends – just maybe.

Clayton William Perry

Clay Perry pulled his saddle blanket up around his shoulders as he looked into the campfire. There were no other sounds on the open prairie except the crackling of the fire and Clay's own breathing. He was tired after the long day's ride and hoped that sleep would come easy; nights before, sleep was all but lost. The solitude of the prairie Clay welcomed, still he'd sleep if possible, with his Colt .45 under his head.

As he watched the flames dance, he remembered each event that had brought him to this night – this star-filled night. Recalling all the things that had happened, they still didn't make any sense – no. Things did not add up. The only thing Clay knew for sure was that five years of his life had been wasted. But why? Why had he been found guilty of something he didn't do?

Now, he was headed back to the town and the people that had caused him more pain and harm than he ever dreamed possible. People whose lies in a court of law had caused him to go through pure hell for five long years.

Clay remembered the hard work that seemed never-ending, the poor food, and the whip – the whip of the head guard that was used at will…. But he needed to think not of the past five years, but the past that put him there. He knew the answer and the reason was back where it all started. And to find those, he must put the prison years behind him once and for all. He couldn't let the pain or hunger cloud his thinking. He must return and find out the truth, yes, return to Ranger, New Mexico. There and only there could the truth be found.

***

The morning sun caught Clay sleeping, and had it not been for a small field mouse running across his bedroll, he would have slept all day long. He rose, stretched, and began poking at the now dead campfire coals. Stirring them, he found a spark; that was all he needed to relight the fire that had become his friend the night before.

Reaching toward his saddle bags, he suddenly found the reason he'd been awakened by the scared field mouse. A rattlesnake lay poised and waiting to strike next to Clay's saddle bags.

Clay didn't move his outstretched hand. Could he retrieve his hand before the snake struck? And what happened to the snake's rattle? Clay thought he had heard these snakes warned a fellow before they would strike, and this one wasn't playing by the rules! But what do to now?

He sat crouched, arm extended, for what seemed like hours. Suddenly, a gunshot, the bullet whizzing past Clay's head. He jumped back and rolled in the prairie grass. Gaining his senses, he first checked his hand. Whew. No snakebite. Then his attention turned to the tall figure sitting the saddle. He raised his hand to block the morning sun and saw a cowboy in a black hat with a full gray beard looking back at him.

"Did he get ya?" the stranger asked.

Clay, getting to his feet, replied, "What?"

The stranger quickly dismounted and grabbed Clay's hand, saying, "Dammit, boy, did the sidewinder get ya?" He examined Clay's hand, nodded and finished, "No. By damn, boy, you're lucky."

Clay replied, "Why, you shot the snake before it could strike, didn't you?"

The stranger turned, walked about ten feet away, then drew his pistol and fired again. "Now he's dead for sure – you know the only good snake is a dead one, and what's best is these rattlers eat real good."

As he added some wood to the fire, the stranger introduced himself. "I'm Dewayne Harden. I run a cattle ranch up on Willow Springs River." Then he added, "Got any coffee?"

"Yes, it's in my saddle bags," Clay said. "Help yourself, and thanks, Mr. Harden. You saved my bacon."

"Think nothing of it. I was just hoping for a meal and some hot coffee."

"Well, all I have is coffee, but you're welcome to all you want! By the way, what did you mean by 'those snakes eat good', Mr. Harden?" Clay asked.

Dewayne grinned and replied, "I'll show ya – you're hungry, ain't ya?"

As Clay watched, Dewayne cleaned the snake by skinning it, then cut it into chunks, putting the chunks of meat on a stick and placing it over the fire. Clay poured some water from his canteen into the tin coffee pot, added coffee, then it set on the fire next to the stick.

The two men sat for a few minutes saying nothing, just watching the fire. Then Dewayne spoke softly. "How long you been out of prison, son?"

Clay was dumfounded. "How did you know?"

"Only a man who has faced the prison whip would have nerves strong enough to wait out a rattlesnake. Besides, I had the same look about twenty-five years ago."

Clay didn't know this man, but he liked him. Liked him right off. The two men drank coffee and ate the snake. Clay found it very filling. Then he said, "I never introduced myself. I'm Clay Perry." The two shook hands.

"So, where ya headed, Clay?"

Clay paused for a moment, then said, "Back to where all my trouble started!"

The look on Dewayne's face let Clay know that he'd listen if Clay wanted to talk. As they drank more coffee Clay talked, talked like he'd known Dewayne all his life.

He told of riding into Ranger about midday, and going, like most men, into the saloon for a drink. After he'd washed down the trail dust, he'd left the saloon and went down the street to a boarding house, got a room and a bath, and then retired for the night.

"Next thing I knew I was awakened about three in the morning by a crowd of people, kicking in the door and beating me with fists and pistols. I woke up in the city jail with a doctor tending to my cuts and bruises. I asked why I was in jail and the sheriff told me to shut up and let the doc work on me," Clay revealed.

"After the doctor finished and left the cell the sheriff returned with another man, who looked at me and said, 'Yes, he's the one. I'll swear to it.' When I asked what the hell was going on the sheriff, Tom Tweat, said I knew why I was there. The fellow he'd brought in owned the dry goods store I was accused of robbing the night before."

Now he looked Dewayne dead in the eye, and stated, "But I'd never seen that man before, and I sure as hell ain't ever robbed nobody, and I told Sheriff Tweat that. He told me to tell it to the judge in the morning."

Clay went on to explain the 'trial' – how the next morning he'd gone before the judge, on trial for robbery. The only witness against him was the store owner, who took the stand and told of seeing Clay enter the store's side door and taking $300 from the store's cash box. Then the sheriff had taken the stand and testified about the arrest and Clay's resisting.

"I wasn't allowed to ask anyone any questions. The jury, all hand-picked by Tweat, only took twenty minutes to find me guilty and sentence me to the state penitentiary for five years," he finished bitterly.

Dewayne was direct. "Did you do it, Clay?"

"Hell no! I was framed!" Clay spat out. "Look, Dewayne, all I want to know is, why? Why did those men lie, and if I was guilty how come they didn't find the money on me or in my things?"

The older man thought for a moment, then said, "Look, Clay, if they railroaded you once, they might do it again. I don't think you need to go looking for trouble. Wanting to know why might land you back in prison. You need to think about that."

Clay looked eye-to-eye at Dewayne, and told him, "I've thought of nothing else for five years, and I can't let it go now."

"Well, if you get there in two days or three weeks, what difference would it make?"

"None, I guess. Why?"

Dewayne smiled. "I've got a ranch one day's ride to the north of here. Come stay with me and think about this thing some more. Besides, you just got out, and you need to relax and forget that hell hole you were in. And I've got the prettiest place in all of New Mexico."

Clay thought about it for a minute. "You won't try to talk me out of it later?"

Dewayne, mounting his horse, said, "Nope."

Clay nodded, then went to saddle his horse and gather up his gear.

After riding for most of the day, Clay spoke up and asked Dewayne, "You said you were locked up about 25 year ago. You know my story. What's yours?"

Dewayne rode on a little way, then with a stone face said, "I killed a man, a man who needed killing. And they still gave me ten years in that hell they call a prison."

Clay did not answer.

The pair rode on, saying nothing. Soon they came on top of a ridge, and down below they were overlooking a large lush meadow. At the far end stood a log cabin with a front porch that ran the full length of the house. Out front was a corral, and next to it a large barn. The barn sat next to a cool, clear mountain creek. Past the creek Clay could see lots of cattle, all fat and in natural grass pasture, belly high.

Dewayne smiled. "Thank God, I'm home. Well, boy, what do you think of this old man's place?"

Clay was wide-eyed as he responded, "I've never in my twenty-four years ever seen any place as pretty as this."

Dewayne and Clay rode to the cabin, where several people waited to greet them. A silver-haired woman who looked to be in her fifties walked down the steps and hugged Dewayne as he dismounted. A man standing on the porch next to a woman, both in their late thirties, spoke to Dewayne, calling him Dad and smiling as he walked up the steps to still more hugs. Then a blond-haired blue-eyed girl in her early twenties called out, "Welcome home, Grandpa."

The older woman was introduced to Clay as Dewayne's wife Helen; the man was James, Dewayne's youngest son, and the lady with him was his wife Paula. Then the meeting that Clay was waiting for came, as was he introduced to Mary Ann, Dewayne's granddaughter. Clay learned later that Mary Ann's parents, Dewayne's oldest son and daughter-in-law, had been killed by Indians when the family first settled the valley.

Both men were taken into the house and sat down to fried chicken, fresh coffee and hot biscuits along with corn, new potatoes and a just baked apple pie. As the men ate, Dewayne explained that everything on the table had been grown or raised there on the ranch.

Clay asked, "With this place giving all of this, and as pretty as it is, why did you ever leave it?"

"I was in Ranger on business," came the reply.

Clay said, "Is the sheriff in town the same one I know?"

"Yes," Dewayne answered, "and before you ask, the storekeeper is there as well."

Clay just smiled for a moment. "Why didn't you tell me?"

Dewayne grinned back. "You didn't ask."

Mary Ann escorted Clay to the bunk house, smiled at the handsome young man, and said, "I'm glad you kept Grandpa company on his trip. We worry about him when he's gone, 'cause he's not as young as he once was."

"Just how old is Dewayne?"

"He's sixty-four, last spring."

She turned at the bunk house door, smiled again, and told him, "Good night, Clay. See you for breakfast, about sunup."

He stood in the doorway and watched Mary Ann walk away, noting each time she looked back at him. He felt a smile come over his face, and murmured, "Yes, good night, Miss Mary Ann."

It was Clay's first night under a roof since his release and he could not explain the feeling, but somehow, he liked it; it felt like home.

Home. Now there was a subject he hadn't thought about in a very long time. Lying down on the bunk and the smell of freshly washed sheets brought back fond memories of growing up in Atlanta, Georgia.

He thought of his mother and father, and the last time he'd seen them. Clay's dad was a good man, a blacksmith, a hard worker and a man respected by the entire city. Clay's mother was a pretty and well-educated woman, a school teacher who like her husband was respected by all.

He remembered sitting in his mother's classroom. In his mind he could see his mom standing at the front of the class reading from Shakespeare and getting his classmates to understand what she was reading. He also recalled his dad's blacksmith shop and the way he worked the steel into wagon wheels and horseshoes. Clay remembered his father's strong arms, could see the muscles flex in them as he heated the raw material in the forge, then beat and formed the material into different shapes. His father was an artist at his trade, the best Clay had ever known.

Clay then tried to reason his wandering ways, his restless want to see new places and meet new experiences. It was that wandering desire that had taken him to the town of Ranger. He remembered his leaving home. Unlike most young men that had to fight to get away, Clay's parents understood his need to explore, his need for adventure, and all they asked of him was that he write from time to time so they would not worry too much.

"Write. Wow," he exclaimed to himself. "I haven't written to those poor people in over five years. I bet they think I'm dead." And he made up his mind. Tomorrow he would write the long overdue letter back home and apologize for waiting so long to write. Yes, tomorrow, but right now he would rest. That was what he needed most. Sleep, and dreams, perhaps of Mary Ann.

***

The next morning Clay was awakened by sunlight coming through the window of the bunk house. He rose, and sat on the edge of his bed, slipping on his pants and boots. Clay then went to the front door and pulled on it to go outside and greet the new day.

The door wouldn't open. It had swelled during the night. Just for a moment Clay's thoughts went back to prison and he remembered all the locked doors, locked so he could not get away, locked to keep him in the living hell he was in.

Suddenly the door gave way and he rushed outside into the fresh morning air. He grabbed the front porch railing, breathing heavily. "They'll pay for locking me up, but first they'll tell me why," he muttered, close to panic.

Then he heard a voice say, "Are you all right?"

Clay replied, "What?" Then his vision cleared, and he could see Mary Ann walking toward him.

She said again, "Are you all right? I was just coming to get you – breakfast is ready."

Clay used the railing to steady himself, and answered, "Yes, I'm okay, I'm just not used to sleeping inside. I'll be okay and I'll be right over. Let me get my shirt," he told her as he turned and went back into the bunk house.

Mary Ann and Clay walked side by side back to the main house, neither one saying much. As they reached the porch, she pointed, saying, "You'll find wash water and a towel over by the pump. Wash up and then come on inside." She continued up the steps, then turned back to him and shyly said, "Oh, by the way, I'm glad you're going to stay with us."

Clay didn't answer aloud as she went inside, but thought to himself *So am I.*

After breakfast, Dewayne asked Clay to go riding with him so he could check the cattle, but Clay knew there was more to the ride. As they rode and Clay was shown some of the most beautiful country he'd ever

seen, he kept turning over in his mind all the reasons
he should listen to the old man.

Old man. Hah! Clay thought. *He's old but wise
and tough as boot leather. I know there's more to this
salty old cowboy than meets the eye.*

After checking what seemed to be a thousand head
of cattle, Dewayne led Clay to a high mountain cabin
that overlooked the entire valley. "Let's stop and fix
something to eat," Dewayne announced as he
dismounted.

"Wow," Clay breathed. "You can see forever up
here, almost to the end of the earth."

Dewayne replied, "Well, it's not that big, but my
place covers three counties and six full sections. We
only covered a part of it today."

The two men made a meal of beef jerky and
biscuits they'd brought from the ranch. While eating
Clay decided to start the talking by learning more about
the man that had saved him from the snake.

"Tell me about your ten years in prison and what
got you there," Clay prompted.

Dewayne sensed that if he revealed his past, he
then might be able to talk some sense into this young
man who was smart but very, very angry.

"The man I killed was my brother. It happened a
long time ago, and what I'm going to tell you will never
be spoken of again – is that understood, Clay?"

Clay just nodded.

Dewayne sat back on the porch of the cabin and
began to talk.

"My brother was names Jerry Don, and best as I
can remember we never could see eye to eye. Jerry Don
was older by two years and I think never liked having to
share things with me growing up. He got to where he'd
lie just to get me into trouble, and he never wanted to
work for things. He learned very young that his size and

strong body would let him just take what he wanted
when he wanted."

"Jerry Don was always in trouble with the law. He
first started stealing some things from the general
store. The storekeeper would catch him and tell our
father, and Dad would punish Jerry Don, but it never
broke him. Soon he turned to bigger things – railroad
payrolls, stage coaches, and the like. But the events
leading up to his death are all that really matter now."

Dewayne sighed deeply, then continued.

"Jerry had gotten caught after a bank job in which
a teller was gunned down in cold blood. Judge couldn't
prove Jerry Don had pulled the trigger, so instead of
hanging him they gave him life in prison. But after two
years, he killed a guard and escaped. I was twenty at the
time and had just married Helen, and the two of us
were trying to build up this place after moving here
from Tennessee."

"Well, one day Jerry Don, still on the run, found
us. But I was gone working cattle at the time, so he
helped himself, as he'd always done, to my best horse
and some money we'd put back. Then he raped and
beat Helen."

His eyes took on a shadow as he spoke. "When I
came back to this very cabin we're at now, I found what
he had done, and after taking care of Helen I took out
after him. He went to a place you know. He went to
Ranger. I followed him and found him in the saloon,
half drunk, bragging about what he'd done. I had
nothing on my mind but getting even. Getting even not
just for what he'd done to my wife, but for all those
years of hell he'd put me and my parents through."

"He was standing at the bar in front of a big mirror
when I walked in carrying my twelve-gauge shotgun.
His back was towards me, but I could see his face in the
mirror. He started to go for his gun, and I shot him in
the back. As he lay dying, cussing me with every death,

I walked over to him, and he said, 'She asked me to do it, she wanted it.' I knew it was a lie, and I pointed the shotgun right at his face and pulled the trigger."

"Clay, the fact that he was an escaped killer and had raped my wife were the only reasons they didn't hang me. I could have gotten the sheriff; I could have done a lot of things different. But I let revenge rule my life and it cost me ten years – the best ten years of my life – away from my wife and sons. Ten years I could have spent raising my sons, seeing them grow up, holding my wife. Ten years. And for what? Killing a man who wasn't worth the dirt on my boots."

"What he did to Helen was real bad, but what he caused me to do was worse. He caused me to be sentenced, not just to ten years of hard labor, but a lifetime of knowing that I let revenge almost ruin my and Helen's life together."

"Now, I ain't sorry for killing him. But I should have let the sheriff do his job. He'd have been tried for what he'd done during his escape, and what he did to my wife, and they would have hung him. He would still be dead. But I let revenge cost both his life and mine, but most importantly time I could have been with my family. Now, being locked up for five years, you know how precious time and life are, don't ya?"

Clay answered, "Yes, I do know. And that's why I must know why I was railroaded out of five years of my life, and by who. Don't you see, Dewayne? I was dead for five years, and now I'm alive again. I'd like to leave it be, but something inside of me just has to find the answer. Finding the answer to 'why' may give me back some of that precious time I lost."

It was late, and a storm was moving in. The two stayed in the cabin that night and talked a while longer, then laid out their bedrolls and called it a night. Clay waited until Dewayne was asleep, then went and opened the front door.

It had begun to rain, one of those slow steady rains, and Clay lay looking out the open door thinking about all that had happened. He remembered the rain being the only thing that kept him going in prison. When it rained all work would stop, and he got to where he prayed for rain every day. But being in a desert setting, it hardly ever rained at the prison; in fact, it had happened only eight times the entire five years he was there.

As the rain lulled him to sleep, Clay's dreams weren't of prison, or of hard times, but of Dewayne's words, and most of all about Mary Ann.

***

Clay awoke, trying to decide which was more beautiful, and being a young man of 24, he chose Mary Ann and hoped he could get to know her better.

Dewayne was already up and had coffee made. Clay could tell that he was in a hurry to get moving and asked, "Why such a hurry, Dewayne?"

Dewayne smiled and replied, "I've been gone from my wife too long already."

Drinking the coffee as they rode, the two started back to the main ranch. Dewayne remarked that if they rushed hard, they might be back around lunch time.

Clay asked, "Dewayne, I don't want to make you mad at me, but would you care if I started seeing Mary Ann?"

Dewayne just smiled and said, "Don't ask me, ask her."

Clay replied, "but you are the head of the house and all I...."

Dewayne stopped him short and said, "Mary Ann is her own boss and has her own mind, but I know what you're saying. However, it's not me you should worry about, it's someone else and that person is tougher than I ever dreamed of being, and if you hurt Mary Ann, I'll just get mad. The other person will kill ya!"

Clay asked, "Who's that?"

Dewayne smiled again, this time even bigger, and

said "Helen."

The two men would ride in silence the rest of the way back now, Clay running through his mind Dewayne's words about Helen and Mary Ann. It stood to reason, seeing as how the two of them had gone through so much together. Still, Clay had feelings for this young, beautiful 20—year—old that he could not deny and now he found himself hoping that she had felt something, too.

The pair arrived back at the ranch about 1:00, and again Helen and Mary Ann were waiting on the front porch. Helen ran to Dewayne and hugged him as he arrived, and Clay, riding a bit behind, said to himself, "I wish Mary Ann would greet me that way."

Dismounting, Clay felt a tug at his arm. He turned and saw Mary Ann smiling; she threw her arms around his broad shoulders and hugged Clay. Clay responded with a huge hug of his own, then he heard himself say to Mary Ann, "I sure missed you, lady!"

Mary Ann showed a little blush now and smiled like Clay had never seen her smile before. One of those smiles a person has when they get the response, or more of a response, than they hoped for.

The couple's hug was broken up by Helen's words, "Lunch is cold; so, you two get washed and come inside."

Clay did not look at Helen but felt her eyes all over his back, and Clay was for the first time, in a long time, afraid of someone - Helen!

After washing up and going inside, while the two were eating Clay and Dewayne overheard Mary Ann say, "Well, our men are back safe and sound."

Helen remarked, "Well, mine is, anyway; time will tell about the other, I guess."

Neither man said a word, just kept their heads down, but now Clay found it hard to swallow.

After lunch Dewayne had Clay help with some branding and de-horning of the yearling stock that had been gathered in the corral. The two worked together like they had worked together all their lives, and Clay was amazed at the old man's physical strength.

Dewayne was impressed by young Clay's knowledge of how to work cattle. Soon all the work was done, and they heard the call for dinner. Clay remarked, "It seems that all the women get to do is cook."

Dewayne smiled that smile of his and said, "That's not all they do, Boy, not at all."

During dinner Clay felt he needed to try to get on Helen's good side, so he remarked on how great the food was and thanked Helen for it. Helen smiled at Clay for the first time and said, "Why thanks, Clay, but I didn't fix it; Mary Ann did."

Clay turned to Mary Ann and said, "Well, I'm impressed - you're not only beautiful but can cook, too – wow!"

Rising from the table, Clay asked if he could help with the dishes. Mary Ann smiled, and Clay felt someone walk up behind him; then he saw something pass in front of his face, and as Helen said, "Hold your arms up," Clay stood very still while Helen tied an apron around the young cowboy.   Then Helen patted Clay on the back and said, "She'll wash - you dry."

Helen then turned to Dewayne and said, "Let's walk like we used to do, Pa."

Dewayne, getting up, just smiled at Clay and Mary Ann as he made his way out the front door.

Helen turned and stuck her head back inside and said, "Don't break any dishes."

Clay replied, "We won't."

Helen said, "I'm talking to you, not Mary Ann, Boy."

Clay again found swallowing very hard as he said, "Yes,

ma'am."

After the dishes were finished - none broken - Clay and Mary Ann went outside and sat on the front porch. They had just small talk at first, about where each had come from and where they had grown up, then Clay said, "Your Grandpa told me about your Mom and Dad; I'm really sorry that happened."

Mary Ann answered, saying, "It was a long time ago and I still miss them; I guess that's the way it is when someone you love goes away. Yes, losing someone you really care about is hard to take, especially when it makes no sense to start with.... I'll bet your parents missed you, while you were in prison."

Clay looked puzzled.

Mary Ann continued, "My Grandpa told me about your problem and said he felt you were railroaded."

Clay smiled and asked, "And what do you think, Miss Mary Ann Harden?"

Mary Ann replied, "What happened to you before we met does not matter at all, but what you do now does matter – it matters a great deal." Mary Ann then reached over and took Clay's hand.

Clay smiled and said, "I've made up my mind to find out why. I know it may not make any sense, but I've got to know why those men took five years of my life!"

Mary Ann held Clay's hand even tighter when she said, "I know, I really do understand; I find myself wanting to know why my parents had to die, but I've got no one I can go and ask! Clay, I don't have any right to say what I'm about to say, but I feel I must say it any way. I've only known you a short time and I may be out of place, but whatever you do please come back to the ranch...I mean, please come back to me."

Clay did not know what to say. A moment passed, then Clay stood and pulled Mary Ann out of her chair and close to him. Holding her in his arms felt wonderful.

He looked into her eyes and with a lump in his throat and a tear in his eye, Clay softly said, "My life is no longer my own; it now belongs to us, you and I, but to have a full life and to have the right to ask you the question I want to ask, I must find the answer and once and for all put this behind me. I promise. I will come back. I'll return to the life I want for you and for myself." Clay then leaned over and softly pressed his lips to Mary Ann's.

The kiss was halted by a voice that Clay had come to respect, when Dewayne said, "My, what a beautiful evening, don't you think, Helen?"

Helen said with a tone of pleasure, "Yes, for everyone, I think."

Clay turned and walked back to the bunk house, for he and all the rest knew he would have to leave in the morning; yes, he would have to make the two—day ride to Ranger to do two things. One, end an old life and so, second, he could start his and Mary Ann's new life.

***

Clay did not sleep at all that night and by dawn had his horse saddled and bed roll rolled up and was ready to go. Just as Clay was ready to climb in the saddle, Mary Ann came out of the house carrying a saddle bag. In the saddle bag she had put enough dried beef, coffee, and other food items to last three men a week.

Handing the saddle bags up to Clay, Mary Ann, with a tear in each eye, said, "Return, my darling...I'll be here for you."

Clay leaned down and again kissed Mary Ann very tenderly. Clay then turned his horse and started up the mountain trail; the same trail that had brought him to the beautiful valley, the same trail that, at the end of, he had found the love of his life, Mary Ann Harden.

Clay rode hard that first day and by night fall found himself only half a day's ride out of Ranger. Clay set up camp and then started to formulate a plan. He knew what he wanted to know; now he needed a plan as to how to get the information. He could not just ride in and ask the storekeeper or the sheriff. After all, they were the ones that had railroaded him in the first place. No, he needed to know why they had done what they had done.

Then he realized something he had not realized before; it was not just the sheriff or just the storekeeper; it was them both. They together had cooked up some type of plan to get rid of Clay, but why? The only answer Clay could come up with was the two must be in on it together. Sure--they both were hiding something, but what?

Clay now knew what he must do. First, he must learn all he could about both men. By learning about the two he would be able to make a connection between the two somehow, and possibly come up with the reason why they had joined forces to railroad him into prison.

Clay knew that any time you wanted to gain information about town leaders, you would ask the one person in town who heard all the gossip and never repeated it. The one person that everyone in town encountered at one time or another, the one person that everybody confided in at one time or another with their deepest, darkest, personal secrets. No, not the bar tender. No, not the preacher.

The only person Clay could think of was a man he had already met. The doctor! Yes, this man knew what troubled everyone around for 50 miles, whether it be medical or emotional, broken bones or whooping cough, and how and why they had it. Clay now knew he must talk to the doctor and get him to reveal as much as possible, if he would!

***

The next morning, he took his time in getting ready to break camp. Clay wanted to reach Ranger about sundown, slip into town without being seen, and then slip into the Doc's office to try and obtain what he felt might be information leading to the question he had asked over and over again in his mind the past five years: Why was he sent to prison for something he did not do?

Clay had noticed the doctor's office on the west side of town, when he was taken to prison, so he rode around the entire town to the north, so he could come in on the west side. It was still early when he reached Ranger, so he waited about a mile west of town, waited for the cover of darkness.

While waiting, Clay tried to figure out what to say to the doctor to get him to reveal what information he had. Clay's thoughts quickly changed to a more positive note, to Mary Ann. He could see her smile and hear her laugh. Clay then marveled at how he could be so very lucky.

Clay's thoughts were interrupted by the sound of a horse's trot. He watched as a lone rider left town and he began to re-think his plan. Darkness was all around him now; it was time to go.

Clay rode into town unnoticed. He reached the front porch of the doctor's house and as he stepped onto the porch, he heard a voice say, "May I be of service, young fellow?" It was the Doc.

Clay pulled his hat down a bit and replied, "Yes, sir, I need to see Doctor Buzz."

The doctor arose from his Chair and went to the front door; opening the door, he said, "Come on in and have a seat over here."

Clay followed the Doc inside, closed the door behind him and sat down in the chair the Doc had pointed to.

"Well, let's have a look at you, the Doctor said as he turned to face Clay. The Doctor paused for a moment, then said, "Well, what's wrong with you?"

Clay then realized the Doctor had not recognized him.

Clay said, "Well, for this treatment, Doc Buzz, you'd better sit down, because the medicine I need to heal me is information. Information I think only you can give me, and I pray that you will."

Doctor Buzz was puzzled but pulled up a chair and began to listen to the young man. As Clay talked, he could see the Doctor's eyes, eyes that said he was going over the files in his mind we call memory. Suddenly the Doc said "Yahoo! Boy, you're the one that was sent to prison for robbing the General Store five years ago. Now I remember ya. You know, I never thought you were guilty. So why are you back here now?"

Clay explained that he had a burning desire to find the truth, and to be able to go on with his life he must put the past behind him; the only way that could be done was to find out what made Sheriff Tom Tweat and Storekeeper Dennis Richard frame him.

The Doc listened as Clay talked on. At one point in the conversation Clay told Doc a few facts that had not been brought out in his trial. Clay recalled that no money was found on him and surely not the $300 that Dennis Richard said he had stolen.

Doc stopped Clay and asked, "What's this about $300?"

"The $300 they said I took from the store," said Clay.

The Doctor now had a look on his face that said he knew something; would he tell Clay?

Doctor Buzz got up from his chair and looked straight at Clay. Doc with a stern face said, "Boy, do you trust me?"

Clay replied, "Yes, sir, that's why I came to you."

Doc said, "Then wait right here, while I go make a house call."

Clay asked, "Where are you going, Doc?"

Again the Doctor said, "You've got to trust me, Clay; I won't tell anyone you're here, but I've got to go see a man; a man that I think can shed some light on this matter; stay here, I'll be back."

Turning towards the front door the Doctor got his coat and hat and started outside.

Clay said, "Please, Doctor, don't hurt me, not like they did!"

Doctor Buzz smiled and said, "As God as my witness, I'll not let anything happen to you, Clay." Doctor Buzz closed the door behind himself and walked up the street towards town as Clay watched from the window.

Doc was gone for what seemed to Clay to be hours. Then Doc returned to his office alone. He went inside and found Clay gone; a few minutes later Clay walked in the front door and just stood looking at Doc.

Doctor Buzz said, "Where were ya?"

Clay smiled, "Outside, watching!"

Doctor Buzz said, "Well, I can't say I blame ya any, the way you were treated around here."

Clay asked, "What did you find out, Doc? Something that will help, I hope?"

Doc Buzz nodded, "Yes, I found out what I feared was true!"

Doctor Buzz sat Clay down and told him a story that after all these years finally made sense to Doc and now would make sense to Clay. Doctor Buzz began talking as Clay listened.

Doc explained, "Ranger was a small town, especially five years ago, and it seems that the Storekeeper had a very demanding wife. About a month before you came to town, Clay, the storekeeper's wife was found outside of town shot to death. The sheriff investigated the matter but never found out who did it. It appeared that someone had broken into the store at night, stole $500 and knocked Dennis Richard out, abducted his wife, then made off with his wife and the money, and later raped her and killed her."

Clay interrupted, "What's this got to do with me?"

Doc exclaimed, "Now wait a minute!... Let's see now, about a year after you were sent up the sheriff bought a pretty little place just south of town, the old Alexander farm. At the time no one thought much about it. The sheriff said he had been saving up for years to get enough money to buy the place. But I know Tom Tweat; I know that he never had saved a dime in his life, or at least not since I've known him and that's been fifteen years. And the man I went to see tonight confirmed what I thought had happened to be true."

Clay asked, "Who did you go see?"

Dr. Buzz replied, "I went to see Sam Perkins, our banker."

Clay was puzzled. "What does this Sam Perkins have to do with it?"

"Well, nothing, except he told me how much the sheriff paid, in cash, for the Alexander farm...$800, the same amount stolen from Dennis Richard's General Store."

Clay asked, "So you figure that Richards paid Tweat to kill his wife for the price of $800; $500 with the first robbery and...."

Doc smiled, "$300 when you came to town; let's face it, if it worked once, it would work again."

As the two men sat talking, suddenly the door to the Doctor's office flew open and standing in the doorway was Sheriff Tweat and his partner in crime, Dennis Richards.

"Think you got it all figured out, do you, Doc?" asked the sheriff.

"Well, I think I'm pretty close to what happened, or should I say what you two made happen," Doc said.

Clay spoke up, "But why frame me?"

Richard stepped in and said, "Boy, you helped us cover the last $300 I owed the sheriff here for ridding me of my wife."

Clay replied, "You paid $800 to have your wife killed?"

The storekeeper smiled. "No, the sheriff ain't cheap, it cost me $1,000, but it would have looked funny to have the same amount stolen again so soon."

Doc spoke up. "That's where you two made your mistake—you two told of $800 total that had been stolen, and that's the same amount Tom paid for his new farm. That's what made me catch on to what you had done."

Clay, knowing that something was about to happen, asked, "What you going to do now, Sheriff?"

Tom Tweat, with a smile, said, "Well, it would appear that you came back to town looking for revenge, 'cause me and the good citizens sent you to prison; and you took poor old Doc here hostage and in the gun fight, well, poor old Doc got shot by your gun. I think my citizens will believe that; I mean, they believed me before, don't you, Dennis?"

The storekeeper answered, "I don't see any problem with that."

Then Tom Tweat raised his pistol and pointed it at Clay. "You're first, Boy, I've got to get your gun and I don't think you're going to just give it to me, are you?"

As the sheriff cooked the hammer back, a shot rang out, but this was not a pistol shot, this was much louder. Doc and Clay hit the floor as Tom Tweat flew forward, a hole in his back the size of a dish pan.

Then Clay heard a voice say, "Get your hands up, Storekeeper," the same voice Clay had grown to respect.

Clay looked up and saw Dewayne standing in the doorway holding his shot gun, as Doc scrambled to see if he could be of any help to Tom Tweat.

"Doc, is he going to make it?" asked Clay.

Doctor Buzz said, "He's dead."

Dewayne told Dennis Richard, "Now as for you, you're going to hang for the paid murder of your wife and what you've done to Clay."

"March to the same jail you locked me up in," said Clay.

Dewayne and Clay escorted the storekeeper to the jail and locked him up as the townspeople gathered in the street.

The next day the judge was summoned from the state capital and would arrive in two days. Dewayne and Clay took a room at the hotel and waited for the judge to arrive for the trial. Clay and Dewayne took those two days to get to know each other better.

After the judge arrived, the trial was held in which every citizen learned of Tom Tweat and Dennis Richard's murderous deeds. Richard was found guilty and sentenced to hang.

The next morning Dewayne and Clay were leaving Ranger when the Banker, Sam Perkins, and a large group of citizens met them outside the hotel.

Sam Perkins walked up on the porch of the hotel and said, "Clay, we know that we did ya wrong five years ago and we can't give you those five years back, but the town would like to make it up to you by giving you this!"

Sam then handed Clay an envelope. Clay looked

inside and counted $500.

Clay said, "I don't know what to say."

Dewayne said, "Say thanks, and let's go home!"

Clay smiled and said, "Thanks, folks. And may God bless each of you!"

Dewayne and Clay mounted up and headed for home. On the ride back Clay talked of his plans to get a place like Dewayne had someday and how he wanted to raise cattle and the like. Then Clay stopped his horse and looked right at Dewayne.

Dewayne stopped and looked back at Clay and said, "Boy, what's on your mind?"

Clay smiled and said, "With Mary Ann's parents being gone, I mean, that makes you her elder, I mean her guardian, right?"

Dewayne smiled, "Yes, I guess it does."

Clay said, "Well Mr. Dewayne Harden, I'm asking your permission to marry your granddaughter, Mary Ann. What do you think about that?"

Dewayne said, "I'll give you my blessing on one condition."

Clay said, "OK, what is it?"

Dewayne, still smiling, said, "That you and she agree to live on the ranch with us. I could use the help, and family means everything, and I'd like to keep mine together."

Clay agreed, and the two men rode on.

***

The next day, they reached the ranch early, and waiting on the porch were the two women they loved more than life itself——Helen and Mary Ann.

Dismounting, Dewayne found Helen's arms around him and once again felt safe. Clay dismounted and not saying a word ran to Mary Ann and held her tight, tighter than ever before.

Mary Ann, trying to catch her breath, asked, "Is your life our life now?"

Clay smiled and then, dropping to one knee, replied, "Only if you will honor me by becoming my wife!"

Mary Ann squealed with joy and delight, and jumping into Clay's arms yelled, "Yes, yes, yes, I'll marry you."

Two days later the entire family was gathered at the cabin, along with some neighbors that lived close by. Helen and Paula had fixed the house up special for the wedding and James had cleaned and pressed his best suit, then loaned it to Clay as his wedding suit. James explained that his brother had used it to get married in, and that he had used it when he married Paula, and now Clay would wear it to become part of the family as well.

As the marriage ceremony got underway, the preacher said, "Do you, Clayton William Perry...."

The wedding was interrupted by Dewayne's laughter as he yelled, "Clayton William! Hell, Boy, I thought your name was Clay!"

The crowd joined in but just for a moment as Dewayne caught the look he was getting from both Helen and Mary Ann.

After the wedding and a short reception, Clay and Mary Ann made their way to the cabin on the mountain top. They would begin their lives together, fresh and under God's eye in the same place where once there was only talk of revenge. Now there would only be love.

Joe Jacobs' Coming Home

As the heat of the West Texas summer beat down on Joe's back and shoulders, he worked steadily at his task. This type of work had become a passion to Joe and filled his days and nights. The work seemed to fill the empty feeling he was now having, feelings he had not felt in eight years. The feeling of being alone, not so much lonely, rather, just being alone. Joe had lost a wife he had spent a lot of time with; they had two children together, but like his wife, they were now gone.

Joe's life had made a lot of changes the past two years, since he had made his way from the big city of Dallas to this small west Texas city of Fabens. The area and climate were new to Joe and that was part of what he liked about his new home. Yes, a new town and a new start, far away from the trouble of his past, trouble he had caused, trouble that had finally caught up to him and cost far more than Joe had ever dreamed the cost might be, his very soul.

Now at the day's end, Joe sat on the front porch of his small house and looked out towards the setting sun. His first thoughts were of the progress he had made on turning this 3,000-acre ranch back into a working cattle ranch. The fence building, the repair of the barns and working pens was going well and the days ahead held promise for a man with dreams of the future.

Then, like most nights, his mind traveled back in time to his past and although he tried to stop the memories, they came rushing back like an uncontrollable tidal wave. Joe could see the faces of his two children and of his wife as he loaded up his wagon then climbed aboard for his trip.

Joe remembered the words his wife spoke as he left. Joe recalled those final words and knew he would not soon forget their sound and their meanings. But what Joe remembered most were the silent faces of the two people he loved most in this world, the faces of his children, Amy and Jessica.

Joe examined the facts that had led to his leaving and reasoned that all the trouble was not his fault. Sure, he was guilty, as guilty as a man could be, having done what he had done. But what troubled Joe most was the fact that no one would listen to the reasons why he had done the things that had led to his being told to leave and not return to the home he had built with his own two hands, not to mention the business he had built from scratch that was now worth about one hundred thousand dollars.

Then Joe looked on the bright side; at least his children would benefit from the store. Yes, their future was secure. They may never thank him for it, but that was alright. He hadn't built the business for their thanks, rather for their future and now that dream was becoming a reality. As for his wife, at this point he could care less for her future. After all, she had pushed him to this night in West Texas. She had lied, cheated, and manipulated her way all their married life and now maybe she would be happy. Joe was sure of one thing – he was a lot better off away from Sarah. Yet tonight for some reason he was lonely.

Then the memory of Kimberly West came into Joe's mind. Kim, as she was known, was a good friend of Sarah's and now looking back Joe realized just how good a friend Kim really was to Sarah. Sarah and Kim had set Joe up, of that he was sure. Now that Joe looked back on the facts it all made sense.

***

Joe remembered that night; yes, the first night it all started. He was working late at the store, putting away a late shipment; in fact, he had already closed for the day and had looked the front door. Joe was working in the rear of the store when suddenly Kim appeared at the side delivery entrance. The door being unlocked, Kim had just walked in and started talking to Joe. Joe recalled telling Kim that his wife had already gone home for the day and suggested that Kim might find her best friend at home. But Kim let Joe know that it was not Sarah she wanted to talk to, but Joe himself. Joe felt this was odd, because Kim in the past had never sought out Joe's advice. Oh, they had talked, but always with Sarah present. Joe knew that Kim and Sarah were always telling their girlish secrets to one another and Joe had never interfered, figuring that the two women were good for each other.

But tonight, things were much different. Kim in the past had always dressed like a lady, never revealing her womanly self in any way to any man, especially not to Joe, but now here she was standing in front of Joe late in the evening, her dress pulled down around her shoulders and the once high neck line now was low enough to show not only her soft white shoulders but also the top area of each breast.

Joe asked, "What do you want to talk to me about, Kim?"

Kim replied, "Now Joe, don't try to act like you haven't been looking in my direction."

Joe replied, "Looking in your direction? What does that mean?"

Kim, sitting down in a chair and pulling up her dress, exposing her ankles, laughed and said, "Now, Joe, I've seen you watching me when silly old Sarah was not looking and besides, Sarah tells me everything; so I know you two are not getting along and haven't been for some time."

What Kim said was true; he had been having trouble in his marriage, but it wasn't anything that he hadn't experienced with Sarah before. Sarah was or seemed to be interested in only two things - money first and being in control second.

Had Kim noticed this characteristic of Sarah as well, and did Kim now figure Joe was ready to venture off into a new, although shady, relationship? What was Kim doing? Joe felt he'd play along and find out.

Joe, looking at Kim, stated, "So you guess me to be ready to, shall we say, try greener pastures, Kim?"

Kim laughed again and leaning forward to give Joe a better view of herself said, "Look, Joe, I'm Sarah's friend, but," Kim was not smiling now, "I've told her she needed to take better care of her man; the one who has taken care of her for so long and had done so well."

Joe did not reply; rather, he just listened.

Kim continued: "I've told her if you were mine, I'd never let you forget how much I loved you and I'd show you every night. No, if you were mine you would not be working this hard this late at night, not in this store room, anyway. I'd make sure of that."

Joe was stunned, but also found himself aroused, and said, "So what would I be doing if you were Sarah?"

Kim arose from the chair, put her arms around Joe's neck, and kissing Joe, replied, "You would be sweating in bed over me, not in this store, Joe!"

Joe pushed Kim away, but only a little. He had to admit it felt good to be number one in a woman's eyes again, even if it wasn't his wife. However, Joe regained his manner and said, "Now Kim, I'm going to pretend that the kiss and what you just said never happened. Yes, I'm unhappy right now but this will pass, and besides, I love my wife, she's a good...."

Kim, cutting Joe off, said with a forceful tone in her voice, "She's a good what, Joe? A good mother, a good and caring wife? Ha! She treats you like a damn slave man and you just keep on taking it. Why?"

Joe, turning away, said, "I don't know, but what I do know is this is not right; it's against all God's teachings and I'd better not let it go any further."

Kim walked over and put her hand on Joe's back. She could feel that his muscles were tense and said, "OK, Joe, but I'll be waiting for you. You're the man I've been looking for all my life and I don't mind waiting. You just let me know when you've had enough."

Kim then turned and walked to the door; looking over her exposed left shoulder she said, "I'll bet you never have been truly loved, have you, Joe?"

Joe did not answer until he had heard the door close, then he said to himself, "True love; what the hell is true love?"

Joe finished his work that night but found the scene with Kim playing repeatedly in his mind. He arrived home about ten-forty-five p.m. and found the children fast asleep. Going to the kitchen Joe found no dinner and began to make himself something to eat. When Sarah entered the kitchen, the look on Sarah's face let Joe know that he was in for a rough go. Sarah demanded to know where Joe had been and who he had been with?

Joe said, "I've been at the store putting up stock and I have not been with any one, dear."

Sarah, yelling, said, "You are lying, Joe, I can see it in your eyes!" Sarah then turned and stomped into the bedroom.

Oddly, Joe's first thought was of Kim and her last words.

After eating, Joe found another surprise. The bedroom door was locked, and Sarah called out, "You'll not get in here tonight, Joe; in fact, you'll not get anything tonight!"

Joe could not keep himself from growing angry and found himself yelling, "Not get anything tonight? Hell, Sarah, I haven't had anything from you at night in months except for a cold shoulder!"

Joe then turned and, finding a blanket, retired to the living room sofa for the night. Sarah was saying something to Joe, but Joe had learned to tune Sarah out and did not listen to her.

***

Joe, still sitting on his front porch, returned to his real world again and had stopped the memory of Kim, if only for a moment.

Joe then noticed a deer about 100 yards away making its way to the watering hole as the evening sun was almost behind Black Mountain. Joe was now at ease and watched as the deer moved without sound. Joe felt calm and at peace. He knew that tonight he would sleep well.

But was the sleep due to the hard day's work at the new ranch or due to the memory of Kimberly West?

***

The sunrise caught Joe sleeping, and pushing his bed covers back, Joe heard what sounded like a wagon stopping outside his cabin. Joe arose and found his pants just in time to hear a knock at the door.

Joe called out, "Just a minute!"

Opening the door, while putting on his shirt, Joe was greeted by Robert Rogers, the local preacher. The preacher was known as "Preacher Bob" by all the townspeople, and he and Joe had first met when Joe had first come to Fabens, but he had not seen Bob in a very long time.

Joe smiled as he said, "Good morning, Bob, come on in and I'll put on some coffee."

Preacher Bob, smiling as always, replied, "Good morning, Brother Joe; and how have you been?"

Now Bob was six foot six inches, most of it all legs, and in two steps was inside the cabin and pulling out a chair at the table while he continued, "Joe, we haven't seen you in church yet, so I figured I'd come out and make sure you weren't dead or something!"

"No, I'm alright, Bob. I just have a lot of work on this old place if I'm going into the cattle business," replied Joe.

"Well, Joe, I guessed as much, but still I like to keep up with folks I like!" said Preacher Bob.

Joe, setting two cups and the coffee pot on the table, said, "Folks you like? I thought a man in your line of work liked everyone!"

Bob just smiled as he poured the coffee into the two cups. "No, not really. I'm human, too, Joe, there are lots of people I just don't care for. Now, I know that Jesus said to love everybody, but I sure find it hard to sometimes, don't you?"

Joe, sipping his coffee, replied, "I find it hard just loving myself, Bob."

The Preacher sensed a meaning behind Joe's reply. "Do you love yourself, Brother Joe?" asked Bob.

Joe said, "Sometimes yes, but most of the time no, or at least not very much!"

Bob paused for a moment. "A man who does not love himself is a man that feels guilty about something, Joe, and if I can help please let me. I'm a real good listener and I know the Bible pretty good. Whatever it is I'll show you what the Good Book says about it. I'll help my brother Joe to love himself again. OK?"

Joe felt he could talk to Bob and found himself wanting to talk, but not now, not yet. So, Joe just said, "Thanks, Preacher Bob, I'll remember that."

The two men sat drinking their morning coffee and were enjoying just being in each other's company.

Then Preacher Bob said, "The reason I drove out this morning was to give you a special invite to Sunday morning's service tomorrow; we're going to have a picnic on the church grounds tomorrow after service and I sure would like to see you come and join us."

Joe, having been alone now for several months, said, "You know, Bob, that sounds like a real good time. I'll be there; what time and what do I bring?"

Bob, smiling even bigger now, "Noon, and just bring yourself, my brother."

Joe, smiling as well, replied, "Twelve noon it is; I'll be there!"

Bob finished his coffee, shook Joe's hand and as quickly as he had arrived was back in his buck board and almost out of sight by the time Joe noticed that he was still smiling at Bob's surprise visit.

The day's work went by very fast and Joe found himself looking forward to the Sunday services and the picnic, but most of all he looked forward to hearing Bob speak.

***

So, at sunup, Joe was up, fixed his breakfast, and went to the watering hole for a bath. Looking into the water he noticed for the first time a full growth of hair on his face. Joe had always been a clean-shaven man and his reflection in the water took him by surprise. Joe decided that a special event like the Sunday service and picnic deserved a new clean look, so he painfully shaved off what had to have been a full year's growth. Now the reflection showed a young man, a man who had worked hard, by himself for two years but nonetheless a young thirty-year-old old man.

Getting a bath and shave made Joe look, smell, and feel a lot better about himself. Joe returned to his cabin. Then, with his Sunday suit on, went to saddle his horse. Joe was amazed to find his horse standing in the middle of the corral, afraid to come near Joe. After about fifteen minutes, Joe finally caught the animal and all the time he was saddling him felt that the horse was laughing.

Finally, Joe said, "Look, it's me. I know it doesn't look like me or smell like me, but it's me. OK?"

The horse just looked at Joe and Joe could have sworn that the animal was smiling. Joe mounted up and headed down the roads towards town, and for the first time felt that he was headed in the right direction, towards church.

After an hour's ride Joe reached the edge of town. Fabens was small - only about a hundred people lived in town and Joe guessed that they all would be at the service.

Joe rode down the main street, looking at the different businesses. He noticed a small but well stocked general store; it reminded him of his own store back in Dallas. He recalled how he started out in a small store just like the one he was looking at now, and how through hard work he had built it into the major store in all of Dallas County. Joe remembered growing so fast that he had to build on and expand the store twice the first year.

Joe rode on and found the barber shop and bath house, then noticed the bank across the street. Larry Wilson owned the bank, and he was the first person Joe had met when he had come to Fabens two years ago. Joe stopped in front of the bank and was looking at the way the building was built when he heard a voice say, "Checking on your money, Joe?"

Joe looked over his shoulder and saw Larry Wilson and his wife Laura walking towards him. Joe, smiling, replied, "No, I know it's in good hands, Mr. Wilson."

Laura replied, "Mr. Jacobs, are you going to service this morning?"

Joe, sitting up straight in the saddle, said, "Yes, ma'am,

I've been looking forward to hearing Preacher Bob speak."

Laura smiled and said, "I guess you did not know about the church picnic after service?"

"No, ma'am, I was told about the picnic by Preacher Bob on his visit yesterday and I'm looking forward to that as well," Joe replied.

Laura countered, "I guess a single man like yourself gets tired of his own cooking?"

Joe, stepping down from his horse, said, "Yes, ma'am, it seems that all my meals taste alike, and I'm ready for a change!"

Turning, the trio now made their way up the street to the small white church house.

As they passed the local saloon, Laura Wilson stated, "I've not seen you in town in quite a while, Mr. Joe Jacobs."

Joe smiled, "No, my place keeps me pretty busy, Mrs. Wilson."

"Most men alone in this area find their way to the saloon and all its Vices - gambling and drinking, not to mention its female, shall we say, 'companions'," said Laura.

Joe, looking straight down the street, replied, "I don't drink, Mrs. Wilson, and the last woman I had caused me more problems than I'll ever get over in two lifetimes; no! That place doesn't have anything I need, nothing at all."

Laura Wilson just smiled as the trio reached the front of the church. Larry walked up the steps and shook hands with Preacher Bob.

Then Laura shook hands with Bob and said, "Good morning, Reverend."

Bob replied, "Morning, Mrs. Wilson; my, don't you look nice this morning!" Laura just smiled. Bob then extended his hand to Joe and said, "I'm Preacher Robert Rogers, and who may I ask are you, sir?"

Joe smiled, "Well, Bob, we had coffee yesterday morning at my place."

Preacher Bob interrupted Joe. "Well, I swear, I'd have never guessed you'd clean up so nice, Joe. I really did not recognize you; I'm sorry, my brother!"

Joe laughed out loud now and shook Bob's hand, saying, "You should have seen the reaction I got from my horse - it took me fifteen minutes to catch him this morning!" Both men were laughing out loud now and some of the others in line as well.

Joe went inside the church and suddenly felt as if he had walked into the past. Joe had once been a deacon in the church back in Dallas, until his sin had been revealed. Yet he felt good being inside a house of God again.

 Preacher Bob took his place at the front of the church and led in several hymns. Joe surprised himself by remembering all the words to each song. Then Bob began to preach and again Joe was surprised; usually when a preacher had a very large crowd, they tried to preach a hell—fire—and—damnation type sermon, trying to get the people scared enough to run down front at altar call. But Preacher Bob, smiling all the while, spoke of God's never—ending love and forgiveness, and told of His sermon on the mount and of His love even for His accusers who put Him to death.

Preacher Bob talked for about twenty-five minutes and lifted every heart in the crowd with his stories of God's love. Joe found himself waiting for the call to come down front and confess his sins so the congregation could pray for him. Joe was accustomed to this type of "call for forgiveness" in the church he was once a deacon in back in Dallas. But again, to Joe's surprise, this did not happen.

Preacher Bob ended his sermon, led a prayer, then declared, "It's time to eat!" at which time everyone left the church house and gathered outside at the tables that had been set up for the picnic.

As the picnic progressed, people were talking, children played all types of games, Joe noticed that at one table a 42 game was underway; at still another a fun game of Hearts was drawing some attention. Joe then saw Preacher Bob sitting with several people. Joe walked over and listened in.

Soon Joe realized that what Bob had said the day before about his knowledge of the Bible was indeed true. Bob was answering questions from those around him. Bob would listen as the question was asked, then, never opening the Bible, would answer the question in detail, quoting chapter and verse. The person who asked the question would then look up the quoted part and read it aloud. If more explanation was needed, Bob never failed to give additional information. Joe was truly amazed and sat for about two hours watching and listening to the entire gathering.

Finally, the picnic was ending, and people were packing up and heading for home. Joe stayed behind and finally caught Bob alone and said, "Preacher Bob, I've got some questions of my own; when might you have time to sit and talk to me?"

Preacher Bob replied, "Joe, I know you're troubled, my brother, now, I do not know why, but I can see the trouble in your face. In fact, I saw it the first time I ever saw you, so why don't you and I sit down out at your place, day after tomorrow. This will give you time to prepare what you want to ask. Will that be alright?"

Joe thought, then said, "You're right; I do need time to figure out how to tell you what it is I need to confess, so, day after tomorrow will do just fine!"

Joe and Bob shook hands and parted for the evening. As Joe rode home he began to think about how he was going to tell Bob about his past. Joe wondered how Bob would handle the news and if Bob would, in fact, be able to help Joe.

Joe reached his small modest cabin and unsaddled his horse. After taking care of the animal with fresh hay and oats, Joe once again found himself on his front porch watching another beautiful sunset. But unlike nights before, Joe now found himself looking to the future. Joe felt for the first time in a long time he had hope for all the tomorrows yet to come.

Sleep came easy for Joe that night and Joe found himself in the middle of a beautiful dream. Joe's dream was the best he could remember because he dreamed about his children. In Joe's dream the children held no hate for Joe, only love and happiness. He watched as his children played in the front yard; he could hear their laughter and see their smiling faces. Just before Joe awoke, Joe dreamed his children told him that they loved him, and both hugged him and kissed him.

***

Joe awoke not feeling bad because the dream was over, but happy, happy to be starting a new day, a new chapter in his young life. He now had an unexplainable deep hope that he would see his dream come true and somehow, some day, he would be reunited with his children.

Joe went through his day thinking about Bob's pending visit and knowing he would have to face and confess to preacher Bob his dark, well—kept secret. Somehow the dream of his children kept coming back as he worked and finally Joe realized that the Holy Spirit was trying to tell him that when he talked with the man of God to be sure and keep his children in mind.

Joe realized that losing his business, his home, and his wife was all unimportant compared to the loss of his children. Sure, a lot had happened, and a lot of people got hurt, but the only thing the adults had lost, other than their worldly possessions, was each other. The children, on the other hand, had lost the security of a stable home and loving parents that were to have guided the children from birth into adulthood. Yes, the two innocent children, the two loved ones that Joe had left behind, were the victims in this whole terrible ordeal.

Joe remembered the part in the Bible that said, "Forsake not the children to come unto me." Joe now understood what that meant - that Jesus wanted us as adults to raise our children in His house and under His teachings. The teachings of love, kindness, forgiveness; not the teachings of man, like money, power, and greed.

Joe was now ready to talk to Bob and to tell him all he had done, but most of all he must find a way to right the wrong that the children had suffered. And Joe knew the only way that that would happen was by coming clean, then, with Bob's help, following the Lord's direction.

At the end of the day Joe found himself on the porch again and excited about Preacher Bob's pending visit. Joe felt that Bob would be by early and found sleep hard to overcome awaiting Bob's arrival.

***

But sleep did come, and the morning sun found Joe awake and up fixing a special breakfast for a special friend.

Joe walked out of his cabin and onto the front porch. Breakfast of eggs, bacon, and hot biscuits was almost ready when Joe saw Bob's wagon coming down the road. Joe stepped back inside and put a handful of coffee in the coffee pot. While Joe was serving up two plates of food, he heard Bob's wagon stop outside his cabin door.

Joe called out, "You're just in time, Bob, come on in and have a chair." Then Joe turned and saw Bob's smiling face.

Bob pulled out his chair and sat down as Joe placed two plates on the table, then Joe watched as Bob bowed his head and began to pray. Joe followed Bob's move and during the blessing that Bob offered Joe realized it was the first time anyone had prayed in his home. After the prayer Joe said, "Thanks, my friend, having you pray in my house means a lot to me!"

Bob never looked up from the table but began eating. Bob then said, "Joe, don't you pray in your own home?"

Joe replied, "No, I never have; I don't know why. I just haven't!"

Bob waited a moment, then said, "Joe, you have got to be one of the best cooks in the state; man, oh, man, this is good!"

The two men just kept eating until all the eggs, bacon and biscuits were gone. Then Bob sat back and said, "Now, I know I came out here to hear your 'confession', but before we get into your past I feel it only right to let you know about the man you're telling your troubles to. You see, Joe, I've not always been a preacher; no, in fact, I didn't get into doing God's work until about seven years ago. And the man that taught me a lot about the Bible and about God was my cell mate at state prison in New Mexico. As a younger man I thought the only way to have any thing in life was to take it. I did a lot of taking and a lot of lying and a lot of running from the law until one day I got caught."

"At first, I was bitter and tried to hate everybody and everything, but Pop Wilson, my cell mate, was able to calm me down and after listening to him for about a year, what he said made good sense. Pop told me that we are all just passing through this life and we're all headed for a tomorrow that will never end. Pop said this is a test of sorts and how we do on this test we call life is what gets us to a happy, loving eternal tomorrow or a tomorrow filled with pain and never-ending suffering. Well, prison life was all the suffering I needed, so I asked Pop how I could be sure of having a happy loving eternal life and that's when my study of the Bible and God's word began."

"Pop Wilson and I spent the following seven years of every waking moment studying, reading, and praying for God's grace and understanding. Then, one year before my release, old Pop Wilson, my dearest friend in this world, died. He was eighty-three when he left this life and had spent sixty years in prison for murder. James Earl Wilson, as he was known, had killed a senator's wife and because of who she was, he got life in prison without a chance of parole. I'll never forget Pop Wilson and how he changed my life; I loved the old man and I miss him very much."

"So, Brother Joe," Bob asked, smiling, "Now that you know about this old Preacher, do you still want to talk to me?"

Joe just sat for a moment, then spoke up and said, "I sure do; you're the kind of man who can understand what it is that is troubling me."

Bob just smiled as Joe arose from his chair and began to talk.

Joe said, "Well, Bob, it started a long time ago, but from time to time it seems like only yesterday. Due to the lack of physical love at home I began to see a woman named Kimberly West. Kim was my wife's best friend, and now I realize just how good a friend Kim was to Sarah. The first time Kim came to me, I should have realized that I was being set up. But to have a woman as beautiful as Kim interested in me and my lack of love at home, I was more than ready for an affair."

"At first, I rejected Kim's advances, remembering my wedding vows and God's word. But as the days passed and then weeks which turned into months, I became weak in the area of physical love. Sarah had cut me off totally in the bedroom and the more she put me off, the more Kim came onto me. I should have seen the plan from the start, but sometimes I feel like I did not want to see their plan and as long as Kim was giving me more than any one man could stand, I guess I did not care."

Joe took a pause, then continued. "The first time I gave into my lust for Kim was in my store. It was late at night and I was working late, you know, restocking the shelves and taking inventory, when Kim came in and said, 'Had enough rejection yet, Joe?' Kim knew that Sarah and I were not making love and Kim also knew how long I had been without sex. After all, Kim was Sarah's best friend and I should have realized their plan but at that point, I just did not care anymore."

"As Kim walked over to me, I never said a word. I remember taking her by the hand and walking her to the back of the store where I keep the blankets and pillows and some household goods. I remember taking her dress off as she unbuttoned my shirt; all the while our lips never left each other. I remember the sound of her breathing and the way she kept calling my name over and over again. I remember laying Kim down on some blankets as I pulled her undergarments down and she revealed her breasts and then her stomach and then all her womanly features to me. I remember how she smelled, how she looked, how she moved as we became one in our lust. I remember being exhausted from our lovemaking and how Kim would not let me quit. How she kept on moving and touching and calling my name until I was able to continue."

"Later I found myself looking forward to our meetings, and I guess other people noticed how happy I had become. People who came into the store during business hours were all making comments like 'My, you're in a good mood' or 'Love must be great at your house, Joe.' And they were right, love was great – but not at home."

"During this period, which lasted about three months, the more Sarah rejected me the more Kim received me. We would either meet in the back of the store or I could close the store and go to Kim's house. But each time we made love was just like the first. I've never made love to any woman or had any woman make love to me like Kimberly West."

"Now, I knew it was wrong, I knew it was against all of God's teachings, and I loved every second of it. In fact, now that I look back to the night that Sarah caught Kim and I and the night that Kim died, I did not care if Sarah found out."

"Kim and I were at her house and were in the middle of making passionate love when Sarah walked into the bedroom with a gun in her hand. Sarah began cussing me and as she raised the gun to fire the first shot, I pushed Kim away. Sarah's first shot hit me in the left shoulder, but I was able to get to her and we began to fight over the gun. Being wounded from the first shot I became weak and found getting the gun from Sarah almost impossible, until I realized that Kim was standing next to the bed screaming at Sarah to hold up her end of the bargain and kill me."

"I held Sarah very tight by holding her arms down, and while holding Sarah had a laughing Kimberly West tell me that she and Sarah had planned the entire thing - Kim would seduce me, then Sarah would come in and kill me, saying that I had broken into Kim's house and was forcing myself on her when Sarah came in."

"Their plan almost worked, but as we fought over the gun, the gun went off, striking Kim in the face; she was dead before she hit the floor. The shock of Kim's death let me pull the gun from Sarah's hand. That was the only thing that saved my life that night. I can still see Sarah setting on the bedroom floor holding Kim's nude dead body, and while rocking back and forth, Sarah was saying, 'No, no, this was not part of the plan, my beloved Kim.' The only thing that saved me was that Sheriff Joel Hutchinson was out making his rounds about the same time, had heard the first shot, and was standing in the doorway and heard the part about me being set up by Kim and Sarah when the second shot went off - the shot that accidentally killed Kimberly West."

"Later I found out that Sheriff Joel had seen me

and Kim together on several occasions, and he knew
the part about me attacking Kim was not true. But, still,
I was finished in the town of Dallas, in the store
business, and in my church. As far as the outside world
was concerned, I was an adulterer who got caught by
his wife, and during a fight over a gun, my lover was
killed."

He hung his head. "Sarah got the children, the
house, and the store, and since she came after me and
my lover with a gun, she also got to keep her respect in
the community. I got to leave my home, my children,
and my business, in total disgrace and shame. I did get
to bring enough goods and money to start a new life.
Sheriff Joel made sure of that - by telling Sarah that
unless she agreed to let me have the supplies and
money, he would tell what he had witnessed that fateful
night."

Joe then returned to his chair at the table and
continued his confession. "But, Bob, there is more to
my story; what I'm about to tell you now can never be
repeated to a living soul. When I left Dallas Sarah's
final words were how she and Kimberly had become
lovers and how they had been lovers from the very
start. I was shocked, and still from time to time find
myself in disbelief, but Sarah's final words keep coming
back. I keep remembering Kim standing beside the bed
screaming at Sarah to finish the job and kill me as they
had planned."

"Now I'm sure that no one in this world knows the
truth about the final shot, the shot that took Kimberly
West's life that night. Sarah and I were fighting over the
gun when the shot went off. And I know that to this day
Sarah does not realize that just before the shot rang out
and struck Kim in the face that I had taken control of
the gun, and although Sarah's hand was on mine, my
finger was on the trigger and I had pointed the gun in
Kimberly's direction. Bob, it was I that fired the shot
that killed Kimberly West. The gun did not go off by
accident, as everyone else - including Sarah - thought;
only I and God know the truth; and of course, now

you."

Joe now sat stone cold and quiet as a lamb, looking into Bob's face. A long moment of silence covered the space between the two men like a blanket of disbelief. Bob then bowed his head and said a silent prayer. Looking up at Joe, Bob smiled and said, "My dear brother, I must ask you only one question."

Joe, not smiling, replied, "What is it?"

Bob, looking directly into Joe's eyes, asked, "Are you sorry unto your soul for all of your sins, not just killing Kim, but all of your sins, Joe?"

Joe, now with tear—filled eyes, cried out, "Yes, may God forgive me, yes, I'm sorry for my adultery, for my killing in anger, but most of all for hurting and causing hurt to my children." Joe was now on his knees, sobbing as he knelt. "I beg the Lord to forgive me, I repent of my sins, I confess my sins, I cannot go on living this way. Please forgive me, Lord."

Bob stood over Joe, watching Joe cry, and Bob began to weep for his Christian brother. Joe reached out for Bob's hand and the two men cried together. After a long silence Bob helped Joe back into his chair and sat next to Joe.

Bob began to speak to Joe, saying, "Joe, just listen to me and hear me out. The things you've told me are important, but what is more important is that now you've told God. Today you finally did what you needed to do, and that was to confess, not to me, but to your Lord and Savior, Jesus Christ. You also needed to ask His forgiveness for your sinful acts, and you've done that as well. I can show you in the Bible verse after verse where Jesus states over and over again that He will forgive us of our sins and wicked ways; but He also says we must first humble ourselves and become pure in heart and truly sorry for our sins. And my brother, you've done all these things today. Now you must forgive yourself and know that God has already forgiven you."

Joe looked up, and through tear—filled eyes asked, "Forgive myself, how can I forgive myself?"

Bob, now smiling, said, "By living the life of a true born—again Christian, my brother."

Joe suddenly became calm, and said, "You mean by truly living as a faithful man to God's law and work?"

Bob stood and shouted, "Yes, my brother, yes, you've got the idea; God gave you His Son and His forgiveness; now give Him yourself, your life and everything you do!"

Joe was smiling again, then suddenly Joe asked, "But should I tell the Sheriff back in Dallas about the shot that took Kimberly's life?"

Bob, looking at Joe, still smiling, asked, "What good would that do, for your children or yourself? Besides, Joe, would he believe you, would Sarah or anyone else truly believe you?"

Joe thought for a moment, then said, "No, they would not; the only thing it would do would be hurt my children more, and they have been put through enough already."

Bob and Joe spent the remainder of the day together, mostly praying and reading the Bible and just being in each other's company. From time to time Joe would have a question about God's word and Bob would pull out his Bible and show Joe what he felt the answer would be. As the day drew to a close and after Bob had left for home, Joe found himself on the front porch, looking at another beautiful sunset and feeling for the first time in years that he now had a new life, a new beginning, and Joe knew that down deep in his soul was true peace, the kind that only God can give. Still, a small part of Joe worried about his children, but Joe figured that being a parent that was only natural.

***

Joe held up his end of the deal and began to go to church on a regular basis and after several months even became a Sunday School teacher to the young adults. Joe worked very hard every day at being God's messenger and found himself loving his work. Praying had become an everyday thing to Joe and just reading his Bible gave him more and more enjoyment as the months turned into years.

Joe's cattle ranch grew as well and although Joe did not intend for it to happen, it became one of the biggest and most successful in the country.

Then one day Joe was sitting on his front porch and heard a wagon coming down the road. Joe turned and saw his dear friend Bob. Joe also noticed Bob's wife Sally, but Joe could not make out the two other people in the wagon with Bob and Karen. Joe went into his cabin to straighten up a bit, when he heard Bob's wagon stop outside.

Joe came to the front door and said, "Well, my dear brother Bob, you caught me off guard, I was just...."

Joe stopped dead in his tracks. Joe could not believe his eyes; could it be? Yes, it was Amy and Jessica, Joe's two children. They had grown a lot, but sure enough Joe was looking at his two daughters.

Weeping, Joe ran to the side of the wagon. As he looked at their tired but smiling faces, he cried, "Thank God, thank God, my children." Both children flew into Joe's arms and began to hug and kiss their daddy.

Bob and Karen climbed down and Bob, as he was unloading the wagon, began to explain: "Joe, your children arrived on the morning stage; it seems that Sarah has passed away from a fever, so the Sheriff sent the children to you; that is, if you want them."

Joe, holding both children in his arms, replied, "Want them? They are my life; of course, I want them, if they want me!"

The children smiled and both said, "Daddy, we love you, we missed you; please let us stay!"

Bob and Karen helped Joe and the children into the house and Karen began to fix supper for the group. Karen told Joe, "You just help get these children settled in, I'll take care of everything else, Joe Jacobs."

Joe sat holding his two daughters. Then Amy, his oldest daughter, asked, "Dad, are you truly happy that Jessica and I have come to live with you?"

Joe said, "I can only think of one time that I was as happy as I am right now." Leah, his youngest daughter, looked at her father and asked, "Was that when we were born?"

Joe, smiling, replied through tear—filled eyes, "When you two were born, yes, I was very happy but not as happy as when I was reborn into my Savior Jesus Christ."

The trio hugged, and Joe's dream of his children playing in the front yard came true. His children had come home to their father because Joe had come home to our Father.

Booze, Gun, Bible

Ted sat motionless at his kitchen table trying to put into words his feelings. He began to recall the events that had led him to this hot July Texas night and the problems, past and future. The only thing Ted knew for sure was he was tired of the life he had been leading and needed relief badly.

Ted became very upset as the memory of his family and early childhood went passing by like a freight train out of control. Ted first recalled his being frightened by a speeding auto. He remembered crying and then being slapped and told to shut up by his father, the driver of the auto. Ted wondered why he could not have been shown compassion and tenderness, the kind they talked about in church.

Now, that wasn't to say that Ted's childhood had been filled with going to church; rather the opposite could be said. But he remembered the teaching from the few times he did go. Now, at forty-six years of age and with a life filled with pain of past immoral deeds, he was going to try and find the answer to why he had done the things he had done. He must find the answer if he wanted to live the remainder of his life in relative sanity.

Ted then focused again as another childhood recollection came by, but this time it came slowly. He remembered a small helpless baby chicken that was dying and recalled how he was told to dispense of the bird by pulling its head off by his father. Ted took the bird out into the back yard and sat with the baby chick for hours trying to find a way to put an end to the poor thing's suffering, but somehow, he just could not bring himself to do as he had been told.

Ted remembered praying for a way to stop both his and the chick's hurting; then, after hours, the chick died. Ted buried the baby chick and held a service for him. He sang a couple of songs he had heard in church - "The Old Rugged Cross" was one and "Amazing Grace" was the other.

Ted remembered returning to the house and he also remembered the harsh words of his father: "If you'd done like you were told and pulled his head off you would have been back hours ago, you stupid kid."

Ted did not answer but said to himself, "I may be a stupid kid but I'm smart enough to know that killing is wrong." Ted felt good about standing up to his father even if it was only in the silence of a six-year-old boy's heart.

Now, sitting at his own kitchen table, he realized that some of his memories weren't all bad. Although that part in the Bible about "honor thy mother and father" came rushing back from time to time. Ted wondered about honor and questioned if one was to honor or give honor to some one that had not earned it.

Honor - now there was a subject that he knew a lot about, mainly because he felt that he had not received any honor from his parents as a child by the way he had been raised. Some people call it respect; others, honor. Ted liked the word honor; besides, it was in the Bible, and if God had used honor instead of respect, then Ted figured that it must be the better of the two words.

How did he get to this table alone, and how was he going to save his very soul? Ted knew he was in danger, the worst kind of danger a human could be in; the danger of hell fire, damnation for all time.

Ted also knew why he was in danger. He remembered the women he had had sex with and how they made him feel. Yes, he had felt like someone special to each one of them. They put him number one in their lives and he had read this as respect and honor. He was wrong.

In the first place he was dishonored by his actions and had let the Devil work and use him to a no - win point. But he also remembered that he had been dishonored by family long before he had dishonored himself by his sexual adventures.

No excuses! Ted knew the danger before he had his first affair and knew that someday he would have to face the one person on this earth that he could not lie to or kid; he knew he would have to face himself.

Now that time had come, and Ted faced the truth. The truth was he couldn't blame his troubles on anyone else, not at forty-six anyway. When he was younger, maybe, but not as a grown adult. His actions had cost him his pride, his standing in the community, and his family.

Ted knew that after all that had happened there must be an answer and he knew the only place to find that answer was in himself. He also knew that no one knew of his love affairs until he had told on himself. Yes, he had tried to come clean and admitted to his wife and kids the truth about his secret life.

The question still raged in his mind. Why?

Had he lived too far outside of God's world, was that the reason? Was God putting Ted to a test, or was Ted being paid back because of a past life he had lived? The Bible he believed in was not known to teach past lives or prior lives. No, God said in His Bible that one was all the life a person was given, so that could not have been the answer.

Then Ted tried to reason on the root of his problem. It was not God who caused Ted's trouble, but man himself. Ted had learned that on this earth he as a people was responsible for his own actions and his reactions. He must pay for those acts at some point. Ted also knew that God's forgiveness was always without limits. God said, "As many times as you ask, you will receive." So, his confession of wrong doings had already been taken care of by God. Now that does not mean that he could go out and sin then ask God to forgive, then go right back out and commit the same sin over again.

He then realized that people have a lot of faults, but God is without fault. Ted reasoned that God made this a perfect world. He made everything work and function together according to his master plan, from the largest animal to the smallest plant. God had everything working in perfect harmony, except for man. Man was the only thing that God made that had rule and control over everything else on this earth.

The birds in the sky did not pollute their own skies. The animals in the rain forest did not cut down their own trees and build houses and factories and roads; no, man had done all these things. Man was the sole source of all the bad things that have happened to man on this earth. Crime, hunger, pollution, war - all were created by man.

That's when Ted tied the two thoughts together. First, man caused all the problems and, second, man was responsible for his actions, whether it be starting a war, being involved in crime, or in Ted's case, sleeping around with other women.

Ted must finally accept responsibility for his actions, no getting around it, no matter how others had treated him. Ted knew that God was going to judge him for what he had done both to himself and to others, not for what others had done to him.

Ted looked at the items on the kitchen table. There was a gun, a bottle of whiskey, and a Bible. Three roads he could travel down and again, the choice was left up to Ted.

If he picked up the bottle and drank it, it might cause him to forget his troubles for a short time, but when he sobered up again the picture would look the same.

If he picked up the gun and placed it to his head and pulled the trigger, his problems on this earth would be over, but his real problem would have just begun. How would he explain to God that he had destroyed the gift that God had personally given him, his very life?

If he picked up the Bible and used it to the extent that he had used the two items prior to the Bible, use it with the same energy and zeal with which he could use the gun and the bottle, he would have a new life, a new beginning, and would solve all his problems.

Ted, having figured and reasoned for hours that hot Texas July night, slowly picked up the Bible and began to pray and read. Ted just happened to open the Bible to the part that talks about being heavy laden and needing rest. As Ted read, he began to receive the rest his soul needed, and after reading for a short period of time and praying as he read, Ted suddenly felt a hand on his shoulder.

Ted had not heard anyone come in the house and was truly frightened by the touch. Ted slowly turned to face a bright white light. Looking into the light he felt a warm feeling of relief and peace. Then the hand that had touched him became clear to Ted's vision; it was strong but gentle and Ted saw a nail hole in the center of the hand; then a voice said, "Welcome back, my brother, welcome home."

Ted's last act on this earth was an act of obedience and complete trust in his faith and in his God.

When his family returned a few hours later they found Ted sitting at the table, his Bible open and his right hand's index finger on the words, "No man comes unto the Father but by me, I'm the way, the truth, and the light."

There is no problem that men can take to God that He cannot answer-—and sometimes the answer is a trip home. Ted was smiling, happy at last. Or should I say happy forever.

About the Author

James N. Richardson of Arlington, Texas was born in Fort Worth, Texas on September sixth, 1947, and was called Home on July eighth, 2019. He was preceded in death by his parents, W.W. "Bud" Richardson and Mary Jo "Jodie" Richardson, his brother, Gary Wayne Richardson, and his sister, Cynthia Richardson.

He was a loved father, brother, uncle, and friend to many. Through his life he enjoyed many rewarding careers, including serving with pride as a peace officer with the Irving Police Department from 1972 to 1977. He enjoyed his retirement from the workforce by becoming a successful gambler; when he wasn't in the hospital, he was in a casino somewhere playing video poker.

A man of many talents, with a quick wit and infectious laugh, he brought smiles to all those he encountered. He was a fiercely proud and supportive father of two and grandfather of four, and he is loved and missed by many.